# GARDEN
PUBLISHING CO.

www.gardenpublishingco.com

# TEMPORARY INFINITY

AUSTIN LANNING

ISBN 978-0-9966453-8-6
Cover design by Garden Publishing Co./Carling Peck
Interior design by Garden Publishing Co.

Printed in the United States of America.

For Emily Jo Craig and Mallory Ross

# SPECIAL THANKS

Bob Johns, Case Smith, Zach Johnigan Jerod Frank, LJ Del Papa, Mitch Freeman, Darius Ewing - thank you for being leaders of faith in my life that have continuously encouraged me in my walk with Christ.

Rob Hartland - thank you for being a mentor to me, a brother to me, for teaching me so much, and for investing in me. It's a pleasure to walk through life with you.

Mom and Dad - I know our relationships have had their ups and downs as I have gone through so many changes, but thank you for the sacrifices that I may never understand and for the relentless love you show. I'm still learning what it means to be a good son. I apologize for many years I pushed you all away and hope that the future holds redemption for that.

The Moseman and Caldwell family - thank you for walking me through this process and for making my dream a reality. I'm forever grateful for the time and chances you took on me and hope that my work is something that you enjoyed being a part of and are pleased with.

Dr. Greg Borchardt - thank you for being a supportive role in a sometimes-non-supportive school system. Your heart for me often kept me going and pursuing the craziest of endeavors. Thank you for the hope you offer my hometown.

737 Guys - thank you for being my community when I had none. Regardless of my school, you all took me in and I'm forever

grateful for the open arms you stretched and the brotherhood you all offered me. I will never forget our years together.

Dr. Green - Thank you for sticking with me and trying to learn about me when I didn't know myself. What we went through was not a psychologist appointment, but two men creating an open space for vulnerability and friendship. Thank you for not giving up on me and my mental state.

Afshin Ziafat, Ben Stuart, Louis Giglio, C.S. Lewis, Henri Nouwen, and Francis Chan - two of the men I thank here have passed. Out of the others, only Afshin has met me. However, I have read books, listened to podcasts, and heard sermons from all of you. You all have said and written things that have had an impact on my life. I have grown so much from simply observing Christians like all of you doing Christian things.

Calvin and the Servant Leaders - thank you all for your friendship. Thank you for listening to me as I figure out this world of ours. I will be forever grateful for the year we spent running towards Christ together, and I wish you all the best.

Dalton Woolf and Chance King - I miss you two every day. You both were dear friends of mine, and not a day goes by that I don't think about the moments when my life changed forever. I am thankful for your lives and hope that my life would make you both proud. I will see you guys again.

Thank you to all of those that have been dear to me. Many people have found their way into my life and I am thankful for all of them. It has been a long and difficult journey getting to where I am. If you have left my side at any point, I do not blame you. After all, everything in this life is temporary and we all struggle to face the world's realities. But I thank especially those that have stood by me, those who I didn't always appreciate, those who loved me when I didn't want love and showed me what it meant to be a friend. You all are the reason I am here today.

# TABLE OF CONTENTS

# NOTE FROM THE AUTHOR

First, I'd just like to thank you for getting this book and for taking the time to read my work. The following is a book about life, not specifically a story of my life. Yes, there are some parts modeled after real experiences, but often situations occur that were never a part of my life; they are just a metaphor for something personal or inspired by emotions and thoughts. That being said, I hope you don't just read this book and try to match it to my life, look for flaws, or just try to get to the end. I hope you really READ it. Take the time to consider the words and events that I've chosen. More likely than not, you may find yourself identifying with many parts of this story. Because, yes, it is fiction, but like I said it's a book about life. I didn't put anything in there that hasn't happened in this chaotic world of ours. Thank you to all the people that pushed me to keep writing this. I dedicated this book to Mallory Ross and Emily Craig as they have been constant supporters in this process, and I thank my family and friends that have given me the love and memories that equipped me to write this story. Some close to me may be able to even see the events in my life that inspired parts of the story. Every person will interpret this differently and get certain things from it. That's great. I want it to start conversation. Everything is in this book for a reason, just as life is. I want this book to leave a message of hope. I want this book to make the world better than it is. If I can do that, then I did my job. Enjoy.

-Austin

# CHAPTER ONE

*When can this all be over?* I asked myself, as if expecting an answer. This question constantly surged to the forefront of my mind, never realizing the result would always be the same.

I tried to push these thoughts out of my head only to be reminded about the cold. The wind slapped my cheek like a whip; my arms crossed. It was a futile effort to gain warmth. Three quarters of my body was numb, but the part that wasn't continued to march on to an unknown destination. I knew if I didn't reach somewhere I would die from the cold. Although, when I thought about it, maybe that was my fate. It's not like I was destined for great things. Every day I tried to forget my past. I wanted to say that's what made me who I am today, but honestly, I wasn't sure if I liked that person.

I stared down at my feet as I walked, trying to keep my head warm. I studied the torn holes of my sneakers noticing that the holes seemed to almost blend in with the horrible condition of the rest of the shoes. The wind died down for a minute allowing me to glance at what lay ahead. I collapsed in exhaustion and frustration. I had been walking since midnight, yet it (like everything else) accomplished nothing. Nothing – the word that characterized my life. It's all I was or ever would be. As my body lay on the concrete shuddering, I accepted that this would be my last day. It's not like anyone would miss me.

I had no family, no friends, and only a few "business partners" that I wished to leave in the past. However, as my breathing slowed, a part of me hauled my body to its feet. I didn't know why I tried to remain here when every day was torture. Ahead of me was a small gap between two three story buildings. It wasn't a heater by any means, but maybe it could take away the wind.

I half-trudged/half-crawled to the space. After a step be-hind the stone walls I collapsed once more. *Now what? Try to sleep, just hoping my eyes would open again?* My eyes wandered across the street to a closed school with its LED sign scrolling, "December 5, 16º F." A fire escape beckoned subtly from the shadows, its blank metal stairs reaching up into the chill, empty night. I picked myself up off the ground. At least I'd go out on my own terms. I limped over to the fire escape. Slowly, step after step, I made my way to the top story. I stood up on the railing and stared at the street below me. All the pain, all the suffering, all the everything was about to come to an end. I searched the night sky. "God, I don't know if you're there or not, but I've had enough. I don't think you can save me this time."

My feet left the ledge and my body flew through the air--lifeless. The concrete struck my body like a truck.

Normally, people would have a will to give at a time like this. I guess a few crumpled dollars, a pocket knife, and an old McDonald's wrapper wasn't worth the legal hoops. As my breathing slowed, a welcome warmth spread over my body. My eyes closed for what I hoped would be the last time.

---------------------------------------------------------------

My eyes slowly slid open to white light. This is it. *This is my relief.* Then, for a brief moment, I was confused. I'd always heard the white light was usually associated with a heaven of sorts, something I didn't deserve to see for myself. Then again, I don't know what else I expected. I guess I only ever thought about the decision that would bring me to death, not what would come after.

However, as my eyes began to focus on my surroundings, my mind rebelled against what my returning sight revealed. This wasn't heaven, or wherever I would've ended up. This was a hos-pital room.

Wires protruded from my arms and my whole body ached. Slowly, I lifted my head to face a doctor at my bedside. "Good to see you're awake," he said.

I didn't know what was happening There was no way I could be alive. Even if I had lived past the impact, how could they have found me? "You are extremely lucky Mr... ahem what is your name, son? We have no records of you and we didn't find any ID on you."

"Eron Basque," I croaked. Honestly, I think that was the

first time I had said my name in months. Most people regard their last name as a legacy, something to keep going for generations. People want their name to be remembered as great, or at least acceptable by society.

Their name could be what brings them to success, or what creates disaster that they were not even initially a part of. My last name meant neither. There was no legacy left to carry on, no accomplishments attached to it, just a name. I surely hadn't benefited from my ancestry, but then again, it also came with no baggage.

I almost laughed at that thought. No baggage. If I had any more baggage I wouldn't be able to walk.

"Well Mr. Basque, to be honest, I'm not sure how you survived. When these two found you, you were unconscious and you weren't breathing. You were immediately rushed here to the Intensive Care Unit. At first you were declared dead but I guess God wasn't done with you."

I smiled, not able to get my thoughts together. I wasn't necessarily an atheist, but I didn't really know where I stood on God. I didn't really know anything about religion. However, I couldn't just deny a miracle, even though it seemed like a pointless one. Out of all the people that could've been saved from death, why me?

I looked at the two people who found me and didn't know exactly what to say. The man held his gaze sternly with a mask of disapproval. Somehow, I knew this front wasn't all there was to this man. He wouldn't be standing at the foot of my hospital bed if it was. His arms were crossed, putting a crease in an otherwise flawless white button-up shirt and a black tie. Straight, thin lips streaked through his well-groomed black beard. My eyes met his. However, his eyes weren't cold. Behind his mask I sensed genuine concern.

I felt like saying thank you wouldn't be enough. Although, I wasn't sure if this was what I even wanted. I was kind of hoping after the other night I wouldn't have to suffer any longer. Not many people received a second chance, even though many people deserved one. Yet there I was.

As for the other figure within the room, I was taken aback. The usual thoughts in my head tended to linger, but here they were flooded out by something stronger. She leaned against the wall relaxed yet ready for anything. Her dark brown hair fell past her shoulders, flowing like calm river. Her eyes didn't seem to be looking at me but into me. It was almost as if my whole life were written across my skin in ink. Every thought, every challenge, every crack on display. At that moment I screamed at myself to snap out of the trance.

*Why even bother with feelings when they simply make your life worse?* I told myself. Which in all honesty, was true. Emotion was my enemy. Yet, something was drawing me towards her.

I wanted to speak, but no words seemed to be enough. Millions of thoughts ran frantically in my mind, as I was unsure of what would come next.

The man took a step towards me and spoke in a gruff voice, "The name's Jack Bentwell." His voice was stern yet had a hint of kindness added to his words. I began to speak, but he cut me off, "Don't try and talk, just rest. We'll be outside if you need anything." He turned around swiftly and walked towards the door. The girl smiled, then turned and followed.

I knew the thoughts that were beginning to intrude my mind were pointless desires. No matter where I went, or how I disguised my wrong-doings, my past would find me; it always did, and always would. I began to get angry at myself.

If I remained here, nothing beneficial would result. "Nurse," I croaked. She spun around and looked at me with worried eyes. "How long until I can leave?" She nervously slinked over to my bedside, "Oh honey, you won't be mobile for a while. And after you are, you'll have to go through months of therapy. It's going to be a long road to recovery." She thumbed through her paperwork. "So, you don't have any form of identification or people to contact. A guardian? How old are you?"

I tried to shake my head but pain shot up my spine. "No. I'm eighteen."

"Well, with you being eighteen. We'll have to go through some paperwork, but after you're stable you'll be free to go somewhere. But unless you have somewhere to go to, Mr. Bentwell said that his family can take care of you until they can find someone for you."

My heart sank. I was sick of always being a burden. There was nothing I wanted more than to leave that very moment. Those people wouldn't have to take care of me, I wouldn't have to see the girl that instantly reminded me about all of my flaws, and I could save everyone around me from the torture that was my personality. My thoughts resumed the infinite battle that constantly raged on inside of me. I couldn't seem to focus on a thought to save me. That is, except for her.

Whenever my mind came to her, all was well. I began to dream. I had always been a dreamer. I was a man that lived beyond the boundaries of the life that was given to him. This tendency to dream led to a lifetime of disappointment, but it was all I knew how to do. Situations that contained nothing but a perfect fantasy scrolled through like a movie. My imagination gave me a future. A real future. Not a future filled with disappointment and misery, but happiness and love. Love. The word was unfamiliar. I couldn't say whether I had been shown it or not. For that matter, I didn't know if I had ever shown anyone love myself.

However, I felt capable of love. I didn't know how to explain it. My heart surged with the longing for someone to love, someone that could make me feel like an actual person--a life where I was enough. Eventually, all of the jumbled emotions drug me to the edge of exhaustion, and my eyes closed, bringing me a long-sought peace.

-------------------------------------------------------------------

There is always a moment of bewilderment when you first open your eyes where nothing is certain. This time the bewilderment continued after the first moment. I was lying in a room worth more than myself. Around me was a world I didn't recognize. The room overflowed with signs of prosperity. Every piece of furniture seemed to be made of the finest materials. The bed I was lying in was a king size cloud that held my broken body together. In front of the bed was a polished oak dresser. Every aspect of the piece was finely crafted with the utmost care. Everything in the room gave the impression that it was placed perfectly in unison. The bureau was the exception. The wood reminded me of a wise and strong elderly man. A man who normally should be weak by age, but rather was dignified by experience. Something crafted with such an intentionality that another could not be created. Every carving wound its way into a brass handle. Etched at the base of each handle were spots of rust.

Jack interrupted my thoughts, "I see you've taken interest in the bureau. We've been meaning to get rid of it, but I don't know," he faltered. "Something about it has made us want to keep it around." He sat down in the velvet chair by the door with confident authority. "Now son, we have a problem. We've been trying to contact your family, but even after entering your name in the system, no one found anything."

He no longer sported his sleek business suit. In its place was a creaseless polo shirt, khaki shorts, and nice shoes whose worth outweighed the purpose. Even without the intimidating look of our previous encounter, the aura of power still graced his presence. I felt that every sentence I spoke must be perfect, even though I had never lived to impress anyone in my life. I chose my words carefully, "That is correct sir. I have no family."

"Well," he paused. His brow wrinkled in thought. "Until we figure something out, you are welcome to stay with us." I didn't know exactly how to respond. I hated the fact that I had become a charity case. I hated the fact that this man felt obligated to care for me, but I knew this was not the answer he expected.

"Thank you," I croaked. With that he left the room, leaving me alone to an unfamiliar world.

# CHAPTER TWO

The next week was incredible. The luxurious lifestyle that I had seen in others but never understood personally was now my life. Anything that I needed was instantly provided. More money than I had ever made in my life was spent on decorations that served no purpose or on items that had use but were never actually used. It was overwhelming.

However, I knew it wouldn't last forever. Happiness is always temporary. I was laying on the bed the family loaned me when Jack walked in briskly requesting to speak with me.

"So," he began as he tensely sat down in a dark green loveseat. His back remained erect, and his hands interlocked as he spoke his next words with difficulty. "What are your plans for the future? We have lived in the same threshold for a little over a week, yet I know nothing about you, or your past." He pulled up a chair from the wall and took a seat on the edge of the cushion, leaning forward. "So, that brings me to the question, where is it that you are going to return, and to whom are you returning?"

My hands began to lose heat. I knew this question would arise soon, yet I could not find any answer. Truthfully, I didn't know where I was headed either.

I had to answer him. I couldn't rely on this man for the rest of my life. I couldn't rely on anyone. These thoughts fought each other until I simply blurted, "I was about to leave."

Jack's gaze shifted in confusion to the crutches at my bedside, then to the brace around my spine, then back to my trembling face. His questioning eyes soon searched mine. We were both at a loss, and for the same reason. We were pondering who exactly I was. Did I really want to do this on my own?

Part of me wanted his help. I certainly wanted a better

life. Then almost instantly I corrected myself. I did not deserve that life. I deserved to be back out on the streets on the cold pavement again. This man did not deserve the burden of dealing with me. With all this conflict, I held his gaze, shaking and frankly hoping that someone would make the decision for me.

His eyes continued to look into mine; they softened, then they hardened once again as he spoke, "You're staying with us. Today is a Saturday. Next Monday we will have you enrolled in the high school that Amber attends. I'll take care of the paperwork. All you have to do is show up. Okay?"

In that moment, the man who used to scare me looked upon me with true compassion. I bit back anything that I could say that would screw it up and nodded my head. He then stood up, taking a step towards me as if he wanted to say more. But, after a moment's hesitation, he turned around and walked out the door. As soon as silence crept in, so did doubt and worry. I then screamed into the pillow until I collapsed, giving up in exhaustion, and the temporary peace of sleep found me at last.

--------------------------------------------------------------------

My eyes slowly opened to the digital clock on the nightstand. The clock read 1:02 A.M., but my mind began racing before I got past the one. I couldn't stay here. I couldn't pursue an education again. I couldn't face people.

Certainly not when I couldn't even face myself.

I slipped on my shirt and pulled over the hoodie from the bureau. I snatched the crutches propped up against the headboard and began to move as fast as possible. I made my way down the staircase, grimacing with every step.

The foyer was silent, everything at peace. The night had taken over, making everything equal. That's part of why I always loved the night. In the darkness you did not know what a person looked like, who they were, what they'd been through, or how much money they had. In the darkness everyone was the same. Through this oddly comforting darkness I stumbled on. I unlatched the door and almost instantly an alarm sounded. I cursed under my breath, hating myself for not thinking about a wealthy house having any sort of security. However, I couldn't go back. Not now.

I shifted my crutches to each position as fast as possible, my back aching and my breath quickening. My legs became a blur. I lost track of whether or not my crutches were actually hitting the ground. My vision became foggy. After several strides my body began to reach a faster speed than it could sustain.

I couldn't move my crutches fast enough to keep up and I smacked into the stones. I rolled into a center arrangement of foliage and flowers that protruded from the circular driveway, a stark contrast with the explosion of pain now consuming my useless, broken body. With no physical or mental strength, I lay on the freezing ground and tears began to stream down my cheeks. I yelled in frustration and anger. My eyes drifted to the sky. I pleaded with everything I had to a God I had neglected most of my life. "God, if you still give a damn about me, please help me. Please. Please help me. I know I'm an unworthy mess that doesn't deserve to live, but I know there has to be a reason I'm still alive. Please God, give me something to fight for, something to live for."

I sobbed into nothing for several minutes until a gentle hand softened the tense muscles in my trembling arm. I looked up to the beautifully concerned face of Jack's daughter: Amber, he had indirectly stated. Looking at her pained me even greater. She represented all of my pointless desires. I felt like a prisoner looking out at a town square full of people. The feelings of worthlessness increased until I began to cower away from her. "Why are you out here in the cold when you don't have to be?" She questioned.

The truth was: the cold is what I was comfortable with. I had never been anywhere else or believed that an alternative existed for me. I couldn't accept this warm, soft life that I had been offered. It wasn't me. However, I didn't know how to say that to Amber. Her life was complete. She had something I did not: happiness. I didn't want to offend her. I didn't want to hurt her. These people were new in my life, yet I cared about them and what happened to them. I cared. Too much. These people looked at me like a charity case. They would never care for me like I cared for them already. I couldn't stay. I couldn't hurt these people the way I knew, sooner or later, I would.

Without a word I pushed myself off of the pavement, bringing my body to my unsteady feet. I grabbed the scattered crutches and made my way down the dark driveway away from the lights, into the darkness.

"Where are you going?"

I stopped. I sensed her shivering body behind me, concerned and confused. I continued crutching. *"Why* are you going?" I sighed and turned to face her, in tears.

"I don't deserve what you and your family have given me. I deserve to be back on the streets. I deserved to die there in that alleyway. You and your father have found happiness. Don't take that for granted. Having me around will ruin it." I paused, looking at my feet as I knew feelings were about to come out that I had never vocalized. "I'm sick of living as a burden. I'm not a charity case. Yet I've had more in one week than I've had in my whole life." My voice rose to a shout. "Your dad wants to send me to school! There's a reason I'm not in one now. I have no future. Your father trying to give me one is pointless. Just go back inside. Leave me out here where I belong. I'd be a better service to this world if I wasn't in it."

I sat down on the cold stones, my body shaking. Amber walked closer, her fair skin illuminated by the moon. She slowly sat down next to me, looking intently at me, as if trying to give her happiness and heart to me through the brittle air. I continued to shake and cry, not speaking. after a short minute, she took the blanket she had wrapped around her and reached out to wrap it around me as well. I shuddered and laid my head on her slender shoulder.

"Whether you believe me or not, I care about you."

I shuddered once more, mentally and physically exhausted. As my body relaxed and my eyes began to close I whispered, "thank you," and fell asleep, oblivious to the world around me.

-------------------------------------------------------------------------

Every moment from that night I dreaded Monday. However, there was some comfort. There was the fact I had a companion. I didn't think that a person could take away pain, but they could walk with you through it. It's the same reason a mom grabs her boy's hand when he gets a shot. It doesn't take away from what's happening, it just, makes it bearable.

Also, after that night, Amber began to come up to my room to talk. She would begin to ask questions that I never felt comfortable answering. So, in return she began to open up herself. Truthfully, I was jealous of that capability. She was able to talk about her feelings openly and comfortably. She had no worry of what I would think or what would happen with the information. It was breathtaking. The way her hands went into her lap as she told a story. The way her eyes lit up as she talked about something she cared about. The passion in her voice. I wanted to hear her speak every day.

The Sunday before my first day she said she wanted to get me out of the house. As we made our way through the foyer Jack stopped us, "Where are you two going?"

"He's been in the house for over a week now, Dad he needs to get outside!" Jack looked sternly at me, as if waiting for me to crack. After a few moments he nodded his head and watched us exit towards a black Mercedes coupe. As we climbed in the car, I realized how different we really were. Amber probably received her driver's license as soon as she turned sixteen, along with an incredibly luxurious car. She probably played high school sports, went to dances, and went on dates.

All I got was an improvised crash course on driving from a man whose driving ruined his life. The "sports" and "dates" that went on in my upbringing were never enjoyable unless you were on the higher side. I dismissed the thoughts along with the memories they were bound to bring.

As the car came to halt, I quizzically took in the surroundings. She had taken me to highest point of the park that overlooked Lake Timor. In front of us was a grass strip shadowed by trees that led up to a stone bluff. Leading up to the edge was a slab of stone, flat and flawless, up until it stopped, transitioning into treetops. I pondered why a city girl would take me to a place like this out of everywhere in town. Yet, the curiosity made me wonder who this girl really was.

We exited the car and she leisurely walked up to the cliff edge and sat on the stone slab. I cautiously followed. She was gentle and beautiful, like a deer, and I chose every movement carefully as to not make her flee. I sat beside her on the stone as she gazed into the landscape before her. I, however, found her more beautiful than any of the nature around us. The park was God's warmup for His true masterpiece of creation: Amber.

Her voice rose like soft music playing against the backdrop of peaceful sounds. "Sometimes I like to come here and think." She paused, gazing out over the horizon with such a strong curiosity. "When life just gets too much and I can't handle the stress, I come back to where it all began. When everything was so simple."

For once, I could relate to her. In that moment, everything was simple. There was no pressure, no past, no judgement. It was just me and her. And for a split second, I felt peace.

"I'm sorry," I said guiltily. She looked over at me quizzically. I sighed. "You've opened up to me. You've shown me things you wouldn't show just anyone, yet I've spoken so few words in response."

There was so much more I wanted to say in that moment. Feelings that I could not project into words. Every word I spoke I chose carefully. I wanted her to see me for someone that I could never see myself as. Truthfully, I was afraid. Afraid that if the real me were revealed, she would take back anything she had ever thought or said. I felt that way already, like I had not met her expectations, disappointing another person I cared about.

"It's just that, anyone I've ever opened up to has left my life or has changed their view of me. You already indirectly know more than I'd like you to know."

I cringed as those last words came out of my mouth. She sunk back, hurt by the realization that I didn't trust her. I took a sharp breath. I couldn't run again. Desperately I tried to cover my mistakes.

"I didn't mean it like that," I stammered, "I care about you Amber. More than you'll ever know. But it doesn't matter. I don't deserve to have you in my life, but at the same time I need you in it." I tried to hold her gaze with confidence but looking into her confused eyes just made speaking worse. I felt that every error I tried to correct I just deepened. I stopped ranting and tried to regain myself. She continued to gaze at me, the sun reflecting off of her beautifully light skin.

"How can you feel something so strongly about someone that you just met?"

"I-I don't know. I have so many emotions that I don't know what to do with. If I thought for a lot longer I could probably come up with a better explanation. I think sometimes when my mind doesn't have time to make sure everything's perfect my heart just empties whatever is inside. Oftentimes when it happens I want to kick myself in the head for saying it, but then I realize if it came from my heart then it must be something I really feel, whether it makes logical sense or not."

She smiled. "I don't think I can articulate what I'm thinking right now either so I'll try the Eron Basque way of speaking," she laughed. "You need me? You got me." She stood up, brushing the dust off of her jeans. I slowly stood up facing her. In that moment I felt something that I hadn't for as long as I could remember. I felt that everything was going to be okay.

Lanning

# CHAPTER THREE

Walking through the double doors of a high school that Monday was most likely one of the hardest things I'd ever had to do. The hallway was insignificant. It was almost natural. No one knew who I was, and no one cared. I was like a shadow faintly making my way.

Amber didn't exactly walk me through the process. I didn't exactly blame her. Just as I was learning to be part of her life, she was learning more about how to deal with mine. She seemed flawless. I didn't expect her to sacrifice her white palate for my stains.

Finally, I made my way to my first class, crutching through the door, head down. The simple drawstring bag I had asked for slapped against my back with every swing. My status combined with my tardiness (due to the condition of my body) aroused many apprehensive stares. As soon as I entered the room, all eyes were drawn to me. Looks of disapproval, expressions of uncertainty, and unspoken accusations of negligence fired at me like bullets.

I made my way to an empty desk, struggling to slide my splinted leg into place. The guy next to me glanced over. "What happened to your leg? Football?"

I grimaced at my own stupidity. I hadn't actually taken the time to think about the answers to everyone's inevitable questions. My mind raced. "Uh... no, car accident," I lied.

The boy's eyes turned from questioning to compassionate. My mind continued to scramble for words until I added on, mostly to prevent further questions: "Yeah, the part of town I lived in didn't have the best drivers, or the best people. That's pretty much why I'm here."

He nodded his head. "Over in the Eastern part of town?" I nodded. The irony was that wasn't a lie. The truth is that inside my past were troubling tragedies that I did not wish to revisit.

"Oh, by the way, my name is Thomas." He reached out his hand confidently. I slowly responded and returned his gesture, "Eron."

Considering my academic history, schoolwork was easier than expected. Things pieced together within my mind like clockwork. *"You aren't no ordinary kid. There's something special about you. You're gonna go far,"* Cameron had told me years ago. I began to wonder what became of that man. For better or worse he shaped me into who I was. The scar that streaked across his cheek because of me, and the courage that brought him into that situation in the first place. He would always be a part of me. Although, the inaccuracy of his words almost made me laugh. Laugh. Something I couldn't remember doing before.

I looked around at the people in the class. I saw how easily they laughed and smiled, how happiness was the default setting to their programming. I wished I was the same. I wanted to be independent of everything that everyone wanted me to be, yet I longed for the similar characteristics that gave them a sense of belonging.

I made it through the first half of the day quietly and unnoticed. Few people spoke to me, and those who did received the same story as Thomas. If this was to become my new life, things would have to change. But for right now, it was all I could do to remain sane.

Thinking of this place as my new life seemed great yet frightening. This could be a new beginning. No one here knew me or could judge me. They only knew what I told them. A smile began to form on my face. I could be whoever I wanted here, unaffected by the outside world or the past. Yet, part of me held back.

Every time I placed my feet on what I believed to be solid ground, it always gave way. I had no foundation to my life and was afraid to try and start to build one. Running was all I knew how to do. Part of me wanted to face the fear I had been running from. But not now. Not now.

I entered my philosophy class, expecting it to go like the rest. However, as class began, the teacher scanned the room, raising her eyebrows at my face. "Hello there, would you like to introduce yourself?" She asked me. Truthfully, I didn't, but if this was where I would remain, then I couldn't be who I was. I waved at the inquiring class, "Hi my name is Eron Basque. I was homeschooled before this." The class nodded in approval of my answer, and the breath of relief shot out of my lungs.

My mind wandered from the subject being taught as I pieced together my new past. As I became lost in my own imagination, the world around me became irrelevant. As if the life in my head was my happy reality, and the life I was a part of was simply a nightmare that would soon end. My thoughts were soon cut short.

"So, Mr. Basque, why do you think there is war and violence in the world?" I blinked suddenly, scanning the board for any clues to the answer she wished to receive. I sighed, "Everybody at heart is after the same thing, happiness. They want it so desperately they're willing to try to acquire all the money in the world, or gather a country to show them love, or even kill to bring them a temporary satisfaction of power. Anyone would do anything, even take or kill, if it meant finding an eternal happiness."

The teacher looked taken aback by my response. "Well yes, I suppose so."

---

Everything ran smoothly for a while, a rare occurrence. However, my bliss was interrupted by itself. As I stepped into the cafeteria, the underlying emotions began to widen the cracks. The facetious reality I had been feeding myself slipped for just a moment. And that moment turned into realizations.

These people knew nothing about me. Which meant very few of them would want to learn more. I scanned the room. Everyone had their groups, their relationships, their comfort zones. No one wanted to break that. Everyone was content with order, with how it all had been. They opposed change. I was that change this time.

Even people who had been here all along and didn't have a group were ignored because that was easiest for everyone else. I don't know why I expected to just become one of them. I wasn't sure I wanted to. To give up my independence; to give up my true self and feelings; to give up everything I had been through by giving myself a new life. And for what?

I turned around and began to crutch down the halls in

search of something to do, somewhere to be. As I continued down the hall I heard footsteps. Amber rounded the corner, and I immediately ducked into the room nearest to me. It wasn't that I didn't want to see her. I just didn't want to explain myself. I hated always having to explain who I am, why I do the things I do, and why I am the way I am.

I flipped to face the room, only to find it vacant. Around me were instruments of brass, wood, and leather. As I slowly walked through the band hall I ran my hand along the tops of the drums. Everything seemed so familiar, yet so distant; like loved memories that suddenly became important.

I made my way to the end of the room and my eyes rested on a beautifully crafted acoustic guitar. I gingerly reached my hand out, picking it up as though it were a memory. I sat in a plastic chair nearby, genuinely relaxing for the first time in years. My right hand ran its fingers along the strings, wiping off any dust or residue. I closed my eyes, picturing a better time that once existed. For that moment, all was well.

I tenderly removed the pick from the upper strings and began to do something I hadn't done for years. I began to play.

My left hand gently moved from string to string as my right arm swung in time like clockwork as I began to progress with the chords. Every worry cleared my head and my mouth opened to release my emotion in the form of melodious words. There was no prerequisite or limits. I was no one else but who I wanted to be in that moment. My voice followed along to the chords, singing about anything that came to my mind. As I continued further a smile crept across my face. I played until I grew tired. I set the guitar carefully back on its stand.

"Wow."

My head shot up to see Amber at the door watching me with amazement. Immediately, I thought about the words I had sung. "Yet, I love you, in hope that you can be the one to repair my broken self." I sat there unable to find a reasonable explanation.

"Hey, it's okay. It was beautiful," she said reassuringly. Relief hit me like a tidal wave. Part of me was happy she learned about this part of me, part of me was scared. I hated revealing myself. I hated being vulnerable.

"What?" She inquired as I underwent my inner dialogue. "You seem surprised to be having this conversation. Did you think we weren't going to talk to each other here?"

I shrugged my shoulders showing agreement.

"When you came into my life you came into all of it. I don't know what you're used to, but I think if you're living your life trying to please others you're not even living your life – you're living theirs. And who needs two of the same life ya know?"

I met her gaze. "You don't know me..."

"Why do you think we're talking?" She smiled.

The fact that she ignored everything negative brought new hope into my life. I wanted this to work, whatever this was. I wanted her to be the one to take my past and throw it all away. I wanted her to be the one that could fill the void inside me, completing the puzzle at last. I wanted her to be the one to make me new again. I wanted her.

I smiled shyly. "Thank you," I whispered.

--------------------------------------------------------------------

As I slowly made my way through the school, I heard my name being called from down the hall. Thomas ran up behind me and grabbed my shoulder. His dark brown hair tumbled down to his eyebrows as he caught his breath. "Hey," he gasped for air, "You should join athletics." I pursed my lips and looked down at my leg cast, and then back up at him with sarcastic eyes. "Okay, I know that you're hurt now, but it's a great way to get to know the guys and get involved," he reasoned. He smiled at me, raising his hands as if holding up the options. Of course, it wasn't what I had intended, but if this was my life, what did I have to lose?

"Alright," I said hesitantly, nodding my head. I didn't know what to expect. Truthfully, that's why I said yes. I was ready for this. I never considered myself to be athletic, but I think a persuasive part of me just wanted to lose myself in something. Because once you get lost in something, over time you begin to stop searching for a way out.

--------------------------------------------------------------------

Things were slow at first. Athletics was just therapy. I would watch the other guys train while I was stuck strengthening my still broken body. Nevertheless, I still hoped that athletics would become a source of recognition and approval.

School was not the nightmare I had first envisioned, but any semblance of friendship there was just something that lasted between 8:00 A.M. - 3:00 P.M. Faces were friendly within school walls, but as soon as I left I was alone. Being with Amber was just a dream. It seemed that I had conjured this mental idea of what our connection could be. Endless possibilities burst as I knew I couldn't share them with anyone or I would be labeled "crazy." Although I think if everyone saw everyone's thoughts we'd find more similarities than society would want us to think. But that wasn't the case, so I kept my fantasy world to myself. However, over time everything expanded.

Athletics became a release for emotion. I found personal strength in the repetitive exercises. Amber and I grew closer. I felt more comfortable as we continued to experience the world. I had always thought that there was a magic formula to friendship. I thought that there had to be similarities or constant conversation, but Amber showed me that just being together and walking through life with one another was often the only requirements for growth to occur. I began to treat other relationships in a similar way. That process turned unfamiliar faces into friends that I learned to genuinely care for.

I started to walk without crutches again. The back brace was soon unnecessary. I began to feel free. In a fairly small school I began to know everyone. And they knew me. They knew the newly confident and outgoing me. As I became comfortable for the first time I started taking chances. I went from looking at myself as a joke, to making jokes that made everyone laugh. As my health improved I began to find myself excelling in athletics. The company of a team gave me a sense of belonging again. The puzzle that I had begun finally started to match up.

I no longer looked down, hoping that I wouldn't run into anybody. I carried myself with confidence, greeting everyone I saw. I found myself achieving goals. At last I was succeeding. Success.

It was such a small example of it but to me it was everything. I felt like I didn't have to carry around baggage anymore. The past I had created seemed real to me, and so did the person I had become. I was finally someone I wanted to be. I was finally someone I could be proud of.

Amber made it even better. We began to spend a lot of time together outside of just living under the same roof. Whether it was late night talks, a simple breakfast on the weekend, or going back to the bluff in the park, time spent with her made everything I had been through seem worth it. Even her friends started to grow past their suspicions of me. I just told them that she gave me rides because we lived on the same street and only answered what I had to. I began to be comfortable. I felt at home with my new life. I felt at home with her.

She was perfect. She knew more than anyone about me, yet never asked about my past or interrogated me. She was my best friend. She knew how I thought, my true feelings, and truly, who I was. I felt stronger feelings for her than I had for anyone.

I looked forward to the next time I would see her or talk to her. There was no need for pointless text conversations because we both knew we were more than that. We talked about ourselves, our dreams, our desires, and about life in itself.

I loved listening to her speak. The way she would get captivated by her own words and the passion in her speech. I loved hearing her perspective on life and how she thought. The way she would speak about past memories of her family and the overwhelming love she had for everyone that was in her life. And if a child was ever mentioned, there was a rush of compassion and care from her that I knew would one day create the greatest mother to a family. She would speak so intentionally on her desires for the next generation and how she wanted to love and guide each kid towards them. Yet through every vision, her plan never surpassed the idea of a relentless self-sacrificing compassion. When she would begin to speak I would sit back, taking in every word she spoke, paralyzed by her beauty.

I still didn't know where I stood on religion, but I knew her beauty was something only God could create. Everything about her was magnificent. I couldn't find any word created by man that truly described her. The fact that she showed interest in me at all was a miracle in itself.

One of the biggest surprises to me, however, was her father. Jack wasn't just a generous man, but he had become a friend and a father. On nights when nothing else was going on, I would sit in the living room with him and discuss the world around us. He would sit back in his recliner and tell stories of how the city of Titchadesh used to be or elaborate on how work was that day. He never really spoke of his wife or family, but that was all right by me since that was a subject I didn't touch much either.

"Mr. Bentwell, how exactly did you get to a place like this in life: a family, money, a job, stability?" I had asked. He sat back and laughed then thought for a moment. "As bad as you want to succeed, there's going to be a few people, a crowd, a business, and a whole world of people that want to see you fail. But if you want something bad enough, you'll do whatever it takes to get there, without question."

---------------------------------------------------------------------------

On my birthday I walked into the guest room that had become mine and resting on the bedside was an acoustic guitar. The mahogany base of the Martin guitar captured all of my attention. It had already been strung along the rosewood neck, ready to produce elegance. My breath escaped me. Overwhelmed, I made my way to the instrument slowly. I began to roll my hand down its side, feeling unworthy to hold the instrument.

"It's all yours."

I turned around and Jack stood there in the doorway, his arm wrapped around Amber. "She told me you never really liked your birthday, but maybe this will be a good one. She also told me you could play."

I looked at them and smiled sheepishly. "I cannot thank you guys enough," I said passionately "For everything."

It was true. This life I had been living was more than just a temporary solution. I genuinely felt that this place, these people – this was a home. Something I had needed for such a long time.

That guitar soon became a part of me. I spent a large portion of my time alone in the room, playing and writing. The night stand was soon stuffed with bits and pieces of songs I had created. The strings on the guitar became worn. Sometimes Amber would enter, sitting quietly, mesmerized as I played for her.

In my old life, I would have simply stopped playing, overwhelmed by the awkwardness of having someone stare at me as I bared my soul in music. But that's the thing. It wasn't awkward, and I never got nervous. She was not a stranger, or someone I felt I had to impress. She was a part of me that could never just disappear from who I was.

"Why do you love music so much?" She asked one day.

"It's not just music though. It's someone's personal experience. It tells a story. Every note and every word were chosen carefully to fit with each other. Every song is someone's life. The memory is captured in it. In a song, no one is judged, no one is better than someone else. It's someone's emotion at its purest form. I respect that. When I write I feel a connection. I feel that I'm using my pain or love for a genuine purpose--and having a purpose is everything. We all want to feel that we have a purpose."

She smiled at my love for what I was doing. She then calmingly rested her head on my shoulder as I picked the strings. In that moment, all was well. The two things I loved most were active in my life. As soon as I had that thought, I realized something I had just begun to understand. I loved Amber.

I couldn't explain what it was about her. I couldn't explain why I felt so strongly. It just was, and yet, after always wanting a response on every question, I was okay with not having this answer.

I looked at the beautiful woman next to me and pondered how a sorry excuse for a man like me could receive someone so great. I thought back to all the times in my life where I hated life. I reflected on the times that I didn't want to go on. I thought about my many suicidal attempts. What if someone hadn't always walked by? What if those times had been more than just attempts? What if I had given up? I never would've made it here.

Yet, even after all that had happened, she was worth it. All the pain and sorrow. All the grief growing up. All of the hatred. All of the lies. All of the brokenness. It was all worth it.

Lanning

# CHAPTER FOUR

On Friday I walked into the band room. Ever since the day I found the place I had found a home in it. The director loved my desire to learn and play and we had become quick friends.

I tossed my bag by the door and looked up stunned. On the openings of the tubas were paper coverings with letters. Together they spelled out "Prom?" Amber walked out from behind them smiling. I didn't know what to say. I was used to never getting chosen; it was the expectation. The fact that she had chosen me out of everyone, the fact that she wanted me, made my heart fly. I smiled and walked up to her. "Yes," I said through the biggest smile I could remember having. I wrapped her up in my arms, never wanting to let go. Her face buried in my chest, my chin on top of her beautiful brown hair. Uncontainable joy was overflowing from me and I wanted to share it with everyone. It was a joy that I never wanted to leave.

------------------------------------------------------------

It was April, and the day of Prom had come. During the past few months I had taken it upon myself to get a job. Even though things were going better, I couldn't allow myself to rely on the Bentwells for the rest of my life. Honestly, it was miserable. When I was at work, any respect was gone. I understood that the life of a restaurant cook wasn't supposed to be glamorous, but covering for people that didn't show up, being spoken to as less than a person, and earning minimum wage didn't really fit the dream. But the thing is, all of that was still better than just mooching off the Bentwells. Every day, every single day, an elderly woman complained her soup wasn't hot enough, every time a box of dressing would explode all over me, every four-hour shift spent scrubbing a ceiling (not a joke), I knew would be worth it. At my lowest points, I just thought of the day it would all pay off. It kept me going. The countless hours and physical exertion were worth it.

Of course, there were times of doubt. I wondered if I was doing the right thing or if this is what I was meant to do.

On prom night, when I saw Amber walk down those steps, any doubts were swept away. She glided out of her room and I felt insignificant as a goddess approached me. I've never climbed Mt. Everest and looked off of it, but I could only imagine that this is what it felt like. It's the feeling of complete awe that is only felt by the people there. I looked to my right to discover Jack was taken aback as well. His eyes filled with pride. To have raised this woman on his own, I couldn't imagine how he felt. From what Amber had told me, this man had undergone struggles of his own. But in this moment, he knew his hard work had paid off as well.

She came near me and I reached out my arm for her to take. As we walked out the door I still failed to speak. Finally, as we made our way to the door I was able to say, "You look absolutely beautiful." It was more though. It was like listening to a perfectly crafted love song that invokes an emotion that you cannot explain but know distinctly.

We exited the house and before us was the Jet-black corvette I had rented for the weekend. She turned and looked at me, "How?"

I smiled, "It wasn't easy, but it was worth it." Her stunned eyes looked up at me. "All of those nights you were gone, all those weekends I never saw you, it was for this?" I smiled again and nodded. I guess looking back it was atypical behavior for an eighteen-year-old, but when an emotion is strong enough decisions become quite easy.

"It was small price to pay for something priceless." I led her to the passenger seat, opening the door for her. Once she was inside I looked up at the door to Jack standing under the arch. He looked down the driveway at me and gave me a small grin. It didn't matter, because in that moment, I knew that I had his approval. I had approval. I was good enough. I smiled again and got in the car.

The rest of the night didn't seem real. I was never used to things ever going right. This night was perfect. She would talk, and I would sit and listen, never growing tired. Whenever I would reply, she would look at me with the utmost interest, her brown eyes looking into mine.

Then, before I knew it, she was in my arms, on the dance floor, with Dan & Shay playing in the background. *How on Earth did I get here?* I asked myself. As we swayed and I held her, a feeling came to me I had never felt before in my life: happiness. It was indescribable, intangible, overwhelming. I didn't understand it, but I don't think I was meant to.

The music continued. Every note was a memory. Every beat matched my heart. Everything I had been looking for my whole entire life was in my arms. Her slender and delicate body was held together by my arms, yet strength radiated from inside of her. All my life I had been searching for something. Countless and restless nights, thousands of miserable days, a lifetime of pain, all were washed away.

Suddenly, she rested her head on my chest. Everything stopped. I could've taken all the time that ever was, or ever will be, and it wouldn't be enough to marvel at the woman in my arms. As I took in everything she lifted her head. Her eyes looked up at me. I stared into the large pools of brown and realized, this woman was not simply hot, or sassy, or any of the words other guys used to describe the girls they would go crazy for. This woman in my arms was loving, down to earth, elegant. She was innocent, yet she loved adventure. She had stood by my side through the brokenness, and yet here I was, feeling like I was finally good enough for someone.

Sensing the depth of my emotion, she smiled up at me. As I looked at this woman, words came from my mouth that I never thought I would say, "Amber Bentwell, I love you." I had no idea what the word meant, but I threw it out there to be caught.

Her eyes lit up and softened with affection, "I love you too." Her words shocked me. Although, it wasn't just amazement that she could feel that way about me, it was amazement that I believed it. I never considered myself worthy of love or happiness. I didn't deserve it. I wouldn't let anyone love me. I lived in a hollow shell that desired a way out yet didn't think I was worthy of that escape. However, when she spoke those four words, it was like they shattered the shell. I felt her love, I felt her emotions, I felt happy.

I felt happy.

---------------------------------------------------------------

I looked over at her in the passenger seat on the way from the after party. The buzz of everything was still present in my mind. Even my doubtful nature couldn't think of anything that had gone wrong.

I pulled into the driveway of Amber's house and looked in confusion at the entrance. The door was open with the light shining out. In the driveway was a dark sedan. I looked over frantically at Amber to find her at loss as well.

I hopped out of the car and jogged to the doorway. "Mr. Bentwell! Is everything okay?" I entered the house and dropped the keys on the ground. Jack was on the ground of the foyer on his knees, gagged. Behind him were three men. The two men on the sides I did not recognize. However, the man in the middle, the one holding the gun to Jack's head, was all too familiar. The scar I had given him still ran along his cheek all the way to his long brown hair. "What, Eron? Are you not even going to say hi to your old friend Cameron?"

Amber spoke with fear, "Eron who is this man?" I stood there, unable to speak.

"Oh, you still haven't told her?" Cameron raised an inquisitive eyebrow, a grin crept across his face. "Well if you're not going to say anything I will. You see I run a business. Some call it contraband, some call it just a gang, I like to think of it as the same as any other enterprise. We sell what the people want, and if it happens to be illegal that just means a higher demand. As for the gang part, I take that as a compliment. I've turned a business into a family environment. Not many head chiefs can say that. Whatever you want to call it, your little friend Eron's father used to be a part of it."

Amber's eyebrows came together in tense confusion.

"Eron have you not told her about your dad either? You've got to open up buddy!" He laughed sarcastically.

"Anyway, his choices led us to take action. Therefore, when he was out of the picture, we needed Eron to take his place working for me. But what does a business need Jack?"

Jack grumbled without looking up, "Competition."

Cameron smiled. "And of course, all competition has to be taken out."

Cameron walked in front of Jack and closer to me with every sentence held in complete confidence. "Was it my desire for money? Possibly. Did we want to be the only ones selling?

Absolutely. Were we going to let another group beat us at our own game?"

He was now face to face with me, waiting for me to make the slightest move. He sneered, "No we were not. So naturally we wanted to take the upper hand by attacking our primary competition before anyone had a clue what happened. Most businesses settle things with law-suits or just old-fashioned marketing techniques. We like to take a more physical and effective approach. Long story short, things got ugly."

He smiled and gave Amber a friendly punch in the shoulder. My body refrained from doing anything about it. "I'm sorry," I said gently as I looked to her to find an unmet gaze.

Cameron continued increasing in volume, "You wanna tell her about the next part?"

"I-I, I don't think," I stammered. His look of expectation didn't change.

"I-He was fighting the leader of the other gang and I could've ended it," I began.

"I had the gun. I had the shot. But," I faltered, "I couldn't pull the trigger."

He pointed to his cheek, "hence the scar, hence us being here, hence us needing payment," Cameron began to yell, "I lost everything because you couldn't man up. Now you need to know what it feels like to lose everything."

I glanced back to my left to see Amber standing in horror. In front of me Jack remained on his knees, staring at me with a gaze of disappointment and anger. I wasn't sure which hurt worse. He had trusted me, and his trust had been misplaced. I stood there speechless. As the world around me began to crash down, I did the only thing I knew to do. I ran.

My head pounded. My heart raced. My feet sped beneath me as I ran down the desolate street. I ignored the world around me. I was angry, angry with Cameron, but more than that, I was angry with myself. I naively chose to have hope for the first time in my life. I was foolish to hope this could have lasted forever. My life was still filled with the inescapable shattered pieces of what once was.

The wheels of the dark sedan sped towards my location as I ducked into the alley way.

I was a coward. The illusion of strength once radiated from my body like the summer sun, and now all that remained was a dark moon full of craters. I knew that there was no going back. I couldn't change the past. I couldn't control the present. I just kept running in hope I would somehow find a better future. I ached as the depression I had been purging from my life seeped back into the cracks of my heart.

I ran for what felt like an eternity. I would think about slowing down, and as soon as I did the feelings returned, so I would speed back up. I wanted to beat down all the emotions and throw them as far away as I could. Finally, my body reached its limit and I fell on the pavement. All the feelings I had been withholding began to break the surface of my body. I took a moment and gathered myself up to proceed on to wherever I was meant to go, and without really meaning to, stopped at the sight of an unfamiliar building before me.

The moonlight reflected off of the stained-glass windows, giving off a slight illumination in comparison to the darkened night sky. The brick walls towered in front of me. Something compelled me to leave the city nightlife and enter the building. I pulled on the large wooden doors expecting them to be locked, but they swung open as if expecting me.

As my feet entered the building my thoughts were erased. I stared blankly ahead as if the chaos had been left at the door, unable to enter. The few lights from the rafters twinkled, providing enough light to walk. I continued to find my way slowly down the aisle passing the vacant pews. There was no confusion. The fact I hadn't been in a church in my life meant nothing. The fact I didn't know who God was or if he existed had no meaning. All that mattered was the experience I was captured in. My body collapsed at the altar as I shuddered at the feet of the cross. A voice began to present itself in my head, expressing ideas I couldn't comprehend. *There is no need to run, for I am with you.*

"No," I said aloud. "No one is with me. I am alone. I am always alone. It's what I deserve."

*What you deserve is not what you will receive. I have a love for you that you cannot understand. There is more to your life than you could ever know.*

I shook my head in dismay. I could not accept that I had any purpose. I could not fathom that anyone could love me. I believed Amber, but she was gone now. I should be too. No one could love me and I couldn't take this life anymore.

*You may believe you don't deserve love, yet I love you all the same. Nothing you can do will alter my love for you. If you could let go of the pain and anger you feel you could see that. You were not meant to carry this burden alone, for I am here.*

I pressed my chest into the ground, finally giving up. However, this was not the same as what I'd done last winter. I was not giving up on life, I was giving up on life alone.

"Alright God. I don't know what I'm doing, but my life is Yours. Take it. Make it into what I never could. I've messed it up to a point that I can't bring it back. Be the Savior of my life. Save me from myself."

Emotion rushed through my body. Feelings of hope and love flourished through my veins.

As I remained kneeling, a hand gently touched my back. I looked up to see a man gazing down at me with gentle and caring eyes. His wiry salt and pepper colored hair and groomed beard framed a worn face that displayed years of wisdom and hardship. Yet his eyes radiated compassion. He offered his hand to me and we sat on the first row of pews together.

"I'm Pastor Reynolds. What brings you here?" He gazed at me curiously. Normally I would've been apprehensive to a stranger prying open my life, but I was vulnerable. No walls remained around me as my emotions were engraved on my skin. "The name's Eron," I said softly as my weak hand met his firm shake.

"I don't know how to explain anything. My life is a wreck, my mind is mess--I haven't been in a church before. I don't know what to do." I fell back against the wood backing frustrated at my lack of communication. I expected him to continue pressing me, or to give me advice I wouldn't know what to do with.

"That's okay," he said bluntly. I looked up at him quizzically. He continued, "You're not going to know what to do more often than not. We're people, and there's no way we can control this crazy thing called life. That's where God comes in. Where we lack understanding and knowledge, He prevails. Don't struggle to take another step when God is offering to carry you."

I began to understand, yet I didn't know if I could give up everything like that. I was trained to trust no one when I worked for Cameron. That night's events had more than reiterated the lesson. My whole life had ingrained in me that the key to my survival was to depend only on myself, and to always watch my back, not to let someone else do it for me. "Pastor, I don't mean to be rude, but you know nothing of what I've been through." For reasons I could not explain, let alone comprehend, I proceeded to tell the man of the night's events as fast as I could. "The only girl I've ever cared about is gone, and her dad was almost killed because of my twisted past and uncontrollable emotions," I looked up expecting to see a look of confusion and surprise, but Pastor Reynolds's compassionate gaze did not waver.

"You've been through a lot I can tell, but you're not alone no matter what you believe. We've all fallen short. We all have done wrong in our lifetime. We all hurt, just in different ways," he paused. "This girl may mean a lot to you, but she is not the answer you've been searching for. The puzzle piece you are missing only has one fit and that is God. If you try to find your happiness in other things you will find it only temporary."

I exhaled loudly into my cold palms. It all made sense, but to accept that everything I had found happiness in wasn't true was not easy to just embrace on complete and blind faith. I shook my head in frustration. I didn't know what to think anymore. I was tired of thinking. Apprehensively I began to speak, "What do I do?" I felt dumb as the words left my mouth. It all seemed so senseless. I continued, "I see what you're saying, but the problem is still here, and even if she isn't the solution to my problems, she's still the most important thing in my life and I'm nothing without her."

He smiled at me, "Don't you see son? You are something. Regardless of what happens with her, you are a child of God. Whether you lose everything, or gain everything, you are still you and God is still God. If you've been blessed in receiving a person like this in your life, fight for her."

He placed his hand on my shoulder and made sure that I was hearing the words he was saying. "If the best things were easy to get, they wouldn't be the best. You have to fight for them. Be joyous in the testing of your will, for it produces strength. But remember, before you can find others, you need to find yourself."

He gingerly opened my clenched fist. In my palm, he placed a silver cross composed of nails with a silver chain and closed my fingers over the metal tenderly. "If you let go of this frustration you'll realize you know what to do." He stood up slowly and made his way to a back room.

I looked up at the illuminated cross on the wall. My

breathing slowed, and understanding started to take place. My gaze shifted to the leather-bound book sitting next to me. On the book was a yellow Post-It note with a verse reference scribbled in ink. *Luke 18:1*, it read. I was afraid it would lead me to something I did not understand, as there was so much I didn't know, yet I gingerly grabbed the book. I flipped to the first couple pages trying to find the chapter. After a couple minutes I found the page and scanned the text.

I looked back up at the cross and mumbled to myself, *always pray and never give up.*

"Really? That's it?" I shouted sarcastically. Pastor Reynolds, apparently, was no longer in the room. I sighed. "Alright, I don't understand, but let's do it. I did the prayer part. It's time for part two. We're not giving up."

I stood up, tucking the Bible in my coat for reassurance. I looked up to see Pastor Reynolds peeping through the doorway to the back room. He smiled and nodded at me. Without a thought, I smiled back. The thing was, it wasn't a fake courtesy. But genuine happiness had found its way, and love had prevailed.

I turned and ran through the doors. The cool spring evening breeze embraced my body refreshing me. I continued down the steps and ran into the night, ready for whatever came my way.

Lanning

# CHAPTER FIVE

My feet sped through the sleepy town. The nightlife had grown dull as time crept further into the morning I raced past the nearby neighborhoods. Normally, I would have stopped to observe. Curiosity would have drawn me off of my route, but this night found me too preoccupied to consider my surroundings. My mind constantly spun with unnecessary thoughts, crazy ideas, and passionate dreams, leading to a constant distraction from everything around me.

I had never been more focused, yet relaxed. As I continued to run, I passed an alleyway that broke my reverie. I stopped. This area was familiar. I took a step backwards and gazed between the buildings. I saw the rusted staircase and began to walk closer. I knelt down on the concrete, running my fingers along the pavement. As the dust flew through the night air a streak of red appeared. My blood. My past. My attempt to end my life.

I looked up at the night sky. The stars illuminated the alley. As I took in my surroundings, my thoughts began to wander. I wondered if my parents could see me. I wondered if they were proud of me. I sank to the ground as I thought about the memory I had ignored for so long.

*I shivered under the bed frame of the small building I called home. My breathing quickened as I held my small hand over my mouth to disguise the noise. My mother and father burst through the bedroom door, my mother falling on top of the bed I was under. My father turned and tried to bar the door behind him.*

*A burly man shoved the door open sending my father flying. He scrambled to his feet nervously stammering, "Please, please, I didn't mean to say anything I swear. They said they would let my family be free. I had to take the opportunity. Take me, leave my family. Please." The shotgun fired. My dad crumpled to the floor. My mother screamed. She ran to his side. The shotgun fired again. My mother fell down next to my father. Tears streamed down my face and a muffled scream erupted from my throat. The man walked closer, flipping the mattress. My eyes looked up at him terrified.*

*He chuckled. "We could use you," Cameron said pridefully. I screamed in protest. He picked me up in his massive arms and drug me out of the room. I looked back towards the bed for one last look. One last look at my parents. One last look at the life I had once known. I screamed and thrashed, desperate to get away. My feet slammed against the narrow halls as my teardrops crashed onto my father's beloved acoustic guitar which lay broken on the wooden floorboards.*

I moved suddenly, snapping out of the daze. I wiped my cheek as a single tear slowly found its way. My eyes lifted toward the sky. "Not this time," I said to myself.

I shifted my weight onto my feet and continued on. I kept walking and as I reached the crest of the hill the entrance to the park became visible. The shadows from the trees immersed the trails in complete darkness, yet I knew exactly where to go. My stomach churned. Although this was a wistful expenditure, I knew in my heart that I would be right. The dirt and leaves crunched under my feet as I made my way up the trail. After walking silently for a time, I made my way through the trees. I was right.

Amber stood there on the edge of the cliff, looking over Lake Timor in the distance. The moonlight offered a white silhouette around her beautiful body. Everything I had planned to say when I saw her went out the window. I didn't need my guitar, or anything to hide myself. I was done hiding. The world had brought me down for so long, it was time I fought back.

"I messed up," I bellowed. She flipped around instantly. I knew she wanted to be anywhere but there, yet I was going to finish what I started. "I've messed up a lot in my life, but that's the past and I can't change that. What I can change is right now. I've been a fool, a wreck, and a coward. But through all of that I was one thing I could be proud of: yours."

She said nothing, but her face continued to show disappointed dissatisfaction. My mind continued to reel through the things I wanted to say.

"I know I don't deserve you, I don't deserve any of this. Trust me, I want to explain everything; I want to fill in all these empty slots. But honestly, I don't know how to show you who I am when I don't know myself. I'm still learning how this world works, and I'm still learning what it means to love someone, but every day I'm with you I'm getting closer. I've lived my whole life wanting to give up, but I know now it's only because I needed something to fight for, something to live for."

She softened as I spoke, yet as I paused after my thought, her brow furrowed again and she held the corners of her mouth firm as if remembering the pain I caused her.

"I know this doesn't change anything. I endangered you and your father, and I'll never forgive myself for that. But I can't just walk away without trying to make it right. I'm done running. I'm done being afraid of this world around me. I'm done being afraid of myself."

I paused, out of breath and emotion. Despite all I had just revealed, there were an infinite amount of things I felt I still needed to say. My mind churned in search of the correct words. I began to get frustrated, as no words could truly convey the emotions I wanted her to feel. There was no guitar or melody to hide behind. There was no back story to initiate sympathy. Then I realized, it's not the pre-conceived words or speeches that reveal someone's heart, it's the things that are said on impulse or reaction. If someone drops something, is our first reaction to help, walk away, or think about it? If a man hands you a parachute will you search for a better way down, think about it, or jump? It was time to jump.

I exhaled deeply, "Amber Bentwell I don't know what love means," I said as loud as I could. "I told you that because it's the strongest word I can think of to describe how I feel. I may not even be using the word right, but I want to learn what it means. I don't like letting people into my life. I wish there was a proper word for someone that has turned your whole life around, broken down walls, and ignited a passion that can't be extinguished, but there isn't. All I can tell you is that this is real for me. No human mind can put how I feel into a handful of letters but trust me I will die trying. I've been through way too much to pretend I don't believe we are here on this cliff for a reason."

Rain began to sprinkle through the thin canopy leaving

dark stains on our bodies. I felt as if the water itself was washing away all of my fears and carrying them down away from the current moment that I had fought so hard for. I had lost too much, yet I still I had one thing left, and I wasn't about to let it wash away with the rest of my past.

I walked closer to her, holding her waist and pulling in her shivering body close to mine. I looked into her trembling eyes, and saw a familiar perspective: one of hurting, one of pain, one of fear, yet it wasn't coming from me this time. However, this time none of those thoughts mattered. I gave up trying to fight the emotions that had ruled my life, and it was time to use them. Like the bridge of a song, everything had built up and all that was left was to finish what I had started. I leaned in passionately yet delicately.

She pulled back. Her eyes fell, shying away from my shock and shame. I took a step back, embarrassed and confused. My body ached with disappointment and instantly the mental war resumed.

I began to open my mouth then paused. I had spoken too much. I turned around and began to walk away. My feet trampled over leaves that although once brittle, had now become so soft they were weighed down; clinging to the ground as if it were all they had. Her voice stopped me in my tracks.

"You think you're the only one with problems?" She said shakily. I stopped, yet not yielding enough to fully turn around. "You had every opportunity to confront yourself. I can't do this for you. If you shut everyone out, a day will come when no one will want in. I thought I knew you, but apparently there's a lot of information missing.

She continued, "We could've fought this war together. You're not meant to hold all this up on your own. But in order to move this mountain out of your life, you had to clear the way. You pushed everything away to create a space. You pushed me away. Congratulations on making that space, but it's an empty one, except for you. You have to accept that there are some things you can't change. You can't control life."

I sighed. I wanted to argue. I wanted to keep fighting, yet she was right. I bit my tongue and continued to keep my back to her. My fingers brushed over the metal cross around my neck. "Okay, but I am going to fix this; maybe not today, but tomorrow is a new day and I'm going to spend every minute of it making this right."

I took another step and paused once more. "And just know, whether I succeed or fail, I meant what I said. As long as the sun rises, I will love you."

I walked back down the trail by which I had come, the oncoming rain disguising the tears on my face. I trudged through downtown until I arrived at the alley and found a familiar cardboard box. I curled up inside, shutting my eyes as if the darkness the alley provided were the only safe haven from myself.

# CHAPTER SIX

My eyes slowly opened and my heart felt full in the new morning. Thoughts were nonexistent as I took in the rising sun. Then it hit me. Everything from the day before overwhelmed me like a flood of memories. "No," I sternly told myself. It wasn't time for self-pity, it was time to rebuild this broken life of mine.

I stumbled through the barren alleys that I so faintly remembered. A few frustrated moments brought me to my destination. My hand brushed the nailed cross around my neck. I paused. People of all ages made their way past me, consumed in their own lives and Sunday mornings. All these people walking amidst the cold had their own wars. They all had their own reasons for being here, as did I. I took a deep breath and entered the building.

I paced briskly down the aisle and took a spot in the center of the church, in the middle of as many people as I could as to not stick out. Pastor Reynolds took his place at the altar, greeting the congregation. Although this man had shown me great kindness, I still felt guarded.

The service soon began. An opening song played, announcements were given and a series of baptisms occurred. I considered the service to be nothing special until Pastor Reynolds changed tone. "Now, we have a special guest here with us," he stated to the congregation. I looked towards the door expecting someone to confidently walk forward, a light in his or her eyes. Confused, I turned back towards the stage to see his eyes looking directly in mine. "He actually doesn't have a clue he's doing this yet. But sometimes you don't need a worldly confirmation to do something, just the call of the Holy Spirit. Eron would you join us on stage?"

My face became stone. I don't remember making the conscious decision to obey, but somehow, I found myself in front of the altar, once again facing the man whose eyes radiated kindness even as they saw more than most people knew. I looked up at the crowd of strangers. They all looked in confusion at my descrambled appearance, wondering how the Pastor knew me. I returned their stares as if to say, *"I'm as confused as you are."* My gaze shifted again to the Pastor. He simply gave a reassuring smile as a response, yet in that alone I felt he understood more about me than I gave him credit for. I shook my head. He nodded his.

*"What am I supposed to do?"* I whispered to him.

*"Whatever you feel led to."* He answered.

"You've got to be kidding me," I said under my breath. I swear I was still shaking my head as my feet pedaled towards the stage. It suddenly felt as though my mind shut down and my heart began to lead. I turned and noticed an acoustic guitar on the stand. *I've given you reason to sing, you don't need to be afraid,* said the same voice from the previous evening.

I gingerly grabbed the guitar. Instantly, I realized my knowledge of worship songs was non-existent. My hand found itself once again brushing the cross on my chest. The pastor realized my situation and simply pointed at the stand in front of me. A handful of chord charts to worship songs were sitting on the ledge, like a story waiting to be told.

I scanned over the pages and found a David Crowder song I had heard a handful of times at coffee shops.

My hands gently brushed the strings as my lips sang the first words. However, as I continued the words began to resonate. I became confident in that what I was doing was right, regardless of the circumstances. The congregation joined in slowly and hesitantly. Word by word, everyone joined in my confidence. As I reached the end, I let the strumming slowly fade until the only sound in the room was the voices of a bunch of strangers just trying to figure it all out like me.

"This is all that I can say right now. I know it's not much. This is all that I can give, and that's my everything."

Silence rested peacefully on the room. I looked up at Pastor Reynolds for guidance. He strode to where I stood, still clutching the guitar.

Turning to me, he placed his hand on my shoulder. "I

have a feeling God has just fired the starting pistol to your journey. Do you have anything else for us?

My heart began to beat fast and my palms dropped in temperature. Yet, as I looked into his caring eyes I knew I didn't want to let him down. So, I spoke words that I could back up, "Give me a week."

The congregation laughed. I couldn't fathom the faith he had just put in me. He spoke as if he knew something I didn't. He smiled approvingly and patted my back as I made my way back to my seat. I was many things -- a romantic, a disappointment, a hopeful seeker, a discouraged dreamer -- but I was not a liar. I had a week to fill the promise I had so wistfully thrown out into the air.

The fact that I had just performed for the first time had left my mind. Even the life I had outside these walls had lost its meaning. All that mattered was I now had a purpose and I wasn't about to let it go.

After the remainder of the service I walked towards Pastor Reynolds to ask him why he had done what he had done but he was talking to an elderly man in the church.

"Pastor, why in the world did you bring that kid up there, and then offer him the stage, do you even know him?" The man asked astonished.

Pastor Reynolds paused and looked at the man lovingly. "When Jesus spoke in the synagogues the religious leaders objected his appearance and cast him out. Matthew was a tax-collector and was called upon out of nowhere to join and lead the Kingdom. I lead this church based off of conviction and God's will, not tradition. If we lose hope in people what do we have?"

I smiled. Even though I didn't get the references, Pastor Reynolds was standing up for me. I left the premises and headed to the park. I had found myself once there, and I knew I could do it again.

I escalated my pace to a trot, placed my still surging body on the edge of the cliff, and lowered down to a sitting position, allowing my legs to dangle and swing like pistons of an engine. My hand went inside my jacket, searching for its purpose, withdrawing the Bible Pastor Reynolds gave me the night before. I flipped open the pages to its mark and pulled out the sheet of paper that held its page. Delicately, as if the pages would rip at the gust of the wind I tenderly unfolded the paper. My right hand dug through my right pocket and pulled out a half-used pencil, close to the end of its lifespan. The lead tip touched the parchment pressed against my thigh and began to write something I never thought I'd write: a sermon.

------------------------------------------------------------------------

The next day I trudged down the street to the high school. There was no wall between this place and reality anymore. This world was one, and the ignorance was not blissful anymore.

I entered the school from the cold weather and the atmosphere immediately changed. "Hey man! Prom was great right?!" Thomas yelled as he came up to give me a high five.

"Yeah! It was sweet, not gonna lie!" I responded as I put on a smile and the best front I could come up with. It wasn't the same as before. It felt like I had come full circle from when I first began. As if it were my first day, I felt that I had something to hide, something I wasn't allowed to be.

"Hey man I'll catch you later, there's something I gotta do first," I told him. He smiled casually as my hand patted his shoulder in passing. There was a purpose to today. I learned every moment contained this purpose, I just had to find it. If I was to obtain what was truly important, I needed to let go of the rest.

I strode up to the field house. My gaze became fixed on the steps. These steps had been the passage of my acceptance. These steps had ascended me to what I believed to be the highest rank: an athlete. My stride slowed as I neared the head office. I stopped. I began to gaze around at the room that held only a semester of memories, yet it felt like a lifetime. The oxygen inside of me expanded and shrunk with the slowness of the time that it held to. *I attributed so much of my social success to being a part of this program. Plus, I was good at it. If I leave this all behind does this mean all the practices, trainings, and sacrifice were worth nothing?* My hand stopped right before it grabbed the handle in question at its own purpose. The voice I heard Saturday night swept my senses again, *"Just because you aren't holding a trophy doesn't mean you haven't received success. Nothing is ever 'for nothing.' You served your purpose in this house, it is now needed elsewhere. It is finished."*

"I can't accept that," I mumbled back at God. "I've been through too much to lose this too. I can't."

*"You must."*

"I can't."

*"You will."*

"I won't."

*"Grab the door Eron."*

"What if I don't?"

*"You must lose everything to gain everything."*

"That makes no sense. It's been two days, what do you expect from me?"

*"To obey."*

"I didn't choose you to become a slave, God."

*"You didn't just choose me, I chose you. Furthermore, I chose you to bring you out of slavery. To bring you out of your bondage to things like this game, or to these people. I know this seems like something that will matter forever, but it is fleeting, and therefore if your heart lies in what is temporary believing it is forever, then you are bound for disappointment as your heart will only last as long as what it lies in. I am saving you from that."*

I frowned, unsure of how I felt.

*"Put that passion in me and I will never run away. I didn't choose you to gain a slave; I chose you to gain a relationship. Relationships require sacrifice. Would you open this door for Amber?"*

My hand twisted the knob and I swung the door open. My coach spun around in his chair slowly. "What's up, Basque?"

The words began pouring out like a river held back by a raging river. "Coach I'm leaving athletics. I know you took such a gamble on me. You believed in me even though you barely knew me. That means more than you know. I thought this was what I needed. This was my ticket to some destination I felt I had to get to; now I see my course is taking a different turn." His face sunk back with sadness. In this moment I realized this man hadn't just looked at me as an athlete; he cared about me. "I will never forget the times I had and the lessons I've learned. This has meant more than you know. Thank you."

He sunk back in his chair for a moment. "Where will you go?" He asked.

"I-I don't know. But I have to trust that I'm headed in the right direction."

He smiled. "You are. There's more to you than a lot of people know. When you first came here, you were more than a new student. There was something else. I'm still not sure what it is, or who exactly you are; I don't think anyone quite knows that, but you were meant for something great. It makes me sad that this is the end for you here, but I know you'll be alright." He reached out his hand confidently. "Best of luck to you, wherever you go."

I smiled and received his handshake, confirming my decision. My mind was weighed down, but my heart was light as I exited. Regardless of all of the difficult ends, I felt nothing but the joy of a beginning.

---------------------------------------------------------------------------

The days that followed were the strangest I had ever experienced, even over my first days at the high school. I began to stop the confident small talk and stopped coasting through my days. I began to desire more, yet also less. I had more in-depth conversations. I stopped worrying over how I was portrayed or who I was seen as. Mine and Thomas's relationship went from a friendship to a brotherhood through late nights of meaningful conversations while listening to music at the park. He never asked about my past, and I didn't feel like it was even relevant. Consequently, I began to invest in others. The girl next to me in Biology turned into Clarice who loved children, but was afraid of the mother she might turn out to be many years from now. The quarterback of the football team turned into Alexander, the athletic all-star that worried if he was good enough, yet spent his time making others feel that they were good enough.

I began to realize that although I was messed up from things in my life, everyone had a story. No one had the same as mine, but they had stories. The great thing was, these stories were incomplete. Every day a new page was written. With each word the story had a capability to change, twist, and turn, providing an unfathomable array of possible endings. A person's story never truly ends. Even after their lifetime, an epilogue is offered as their life may have had a minor or major role in another's story. However, as Sunday neared, I realized it was time for book number one of mine to be told. I had spent my life living a lie. It was time to tell the truth.

It was Saturday. I walked away from the park where a group of us had been hammocking per usual. The sun had begun to set and the noises of the city were silent as the transition of those that thrive in the day are replaced by the life of the night. However, the silence that used to be the greatest fear within me had grown into a solitude I thrived in. My thoughts were finally allowed to flow. Yet, it was not in distress or a panic that they moved along with, but a smooth control. I was analyzing life in an objective understanding, not a personal frustration.

I chose the long way to my alley as I needed to clear my head. I passed through downtown, observing the empty streets filled with buildings, waiting for occupants to give them a purpose. My stomach growled. Ever since I left the Bentwell's the school meals were my only meals. At the same time, my physical hunger couldn't dampen my new satisfaction with life. Just by sharing my situation with a handful of people, kindness, not food, had become my lifeline. Before my life changed, I had very little hope in humanity. I believed that people were bound to let me down. Now there was hope. People surprised me.

I continued, wandering into the part of town where I grew up if you could call it that.

"Eron, that you?" I heard a familiar voice call after me as I crossed the street. I turned around to see Kyle gazing at me with wide eyes. He was the closest thing I had to a friend when I worked for Cameron. His hair was long and unkempt as it was filled with dirt and grime.

As he stepped into the illuminated circle of a light post, two other familiar faces entered the scene. James's eyes went up slowly to meet mine, "Where ya been man?" His glasses looked worn out as a small crack traced the left lens. I didn't remember that. In fact, I didn't even remember James wearing glasses.

Melanie swayed side to side, her face unable to look at mine. "We thought something had happened to you."

Immediately my heart filled with guilt. I hadn't thought about these people in so long. I had become consumed with my new life. My eyes had finally become set on the future and even the good parts of the past were being thrown away.

James now stared intently at me, reading into my thoughts. "You forgot about us, didn't you?" I searched for a response but found none. I was proud of the words I had written on the paper that I had tucked in my jacket, yet on the spot I was useless. It was as if I had experienced amnesia, and my memory was flooding back for the first time. I remembered the time I broke down in the warehouse after my parents died, and a younger Kyle came over to comfort me.

I remember Melanie meeting me on the old railroad bridge the night I fled from Cameron's empire.

I remembered everything.

*"Eron! Eron!" The voices shouted from the tree line. I sat there in my own tears, the noose trembling in my hands. No sign of strength appeared from my body as I shook in anguish underneath the blackened sky. James ran up, out of breath. "Eron give me that right now!" He yanked the noose from my fingers without struggle. Melanie followed, glancing at the noose in James's hands and then back at me sitting on the ground, tears streaming down my reddened cheeks. "Eron you can't just give up like this, you have more to live for."*

*"And what exactly is that?!" I screamed at them. "All I know is how to run. My life already amounted to nothing, now there's going to be bounty to have it gone. I might as well save them the trouble. Everyone I love is dead and soon I will be, too."*

*"We're not dead," Kyle pointed out glumly breaking the silence of the group. Melanie crouched down beside me grabbing my shoulder, the other two following suit.*

*"Life sucks---for all of us. But for some reason we're not dead. For some reason we were given each other. If that doesn't mean something I don't know what does. If you give up your life, you're giving up ours too. We're in this together." My eyes hesitantly lifted to Melanie's. I nodded in approval of her statement.*

*"Even when you mean nothing to yourself, you still mean something to us," Kyle pointed out. I stared at the matted grass. I didn't know if I believed that. Why would anyone care about my non-important life? James noticed this frustration and shook my shoulders. "Eron snap out of it. So what if you left Cameron at the mercy of some maniac, he probably deserved it. It's over now, and throwing away your life isn't the way to change it. I know you want change. I know you want a better life. We all do. But this piece of rope on a tree branch isn't going to solve any of those problems. You're gonna make it past this, we all are." He proceeded to grab my arm and pull me up to my feet. Melanie embraced me. The two guys shrugged and joined in as I shuddered with emotion. We were going to be okay.*

James was right that night. I would make it through. But now, the roles were reversed. As I looked at their tattered jackets and worn out sneakers, I realized I could have done something about their state. I didn't. I had left their company the night I had attempted to end my life once more. Yet somehow, I was the one that made it out. I didn't deserve that.

"I don't know what to say." I never appreciated these people like I should've, even though they were the reason I was standing there.

"You look to be doing well," Kyle pointed out. I looked down at myself. I hadn't changed since the past Saturday and had worn the same clothes the whole week. The only people that asked were the ones that knew my situation so I didn't feel the need to change it. Even so, the khaki pants and nice t-shirt I was wearing was better than anything they had. I considered myself the victim of society because my bed was a box, but I was blessed compared to the people in front of me.

"There's a lot of things I want to say to you guys, and a lot of apologizing that needs to take place, but I think there's a better way to convey that message. Follow me."

The three friends looked at each other with mixed emotions then shrugged. "Okay," James said grudgingly, "lead the way."

I looked at them amazedly. I didn't expect them to agree or comply, at least not without an argument, but once again I was given a grace I didn't deserve. I gave a small smile and turned towards the church and began walking.

We hadn't seen each other in months, but the walk was one taken in silence. When we arrived I took a seat under the streetlight. "We have to wait until morning." They hesitantly took a seat and laid down. I pulled the journal out of my jacket and scratched out everything I had written in the past week. I marked out every clever construction and every logical claim and began to write my life story.

Lanning

# CHAPTER SEVEN

"Well hello," Pastor Reynolds said as my eyes opened to the bright sunlight of the Sunday morning. We all slowly sat up and adjusted to the light. I didn't really think about what an odd sight four essentially homeless kids sleeping at the corner of a church would be. Pastor Reynolds simply smiled at us as if nothing was wrong.

I smiled sheepishly. "Come on in whenever you're ready, you still have time," he assured me. He stood up confidently brushing the dust off of his slacks as he turned and stepped inside leaving me and my companions on the steps.

"That man knew who you were? Do you go to church here? I never even knew you went for all that stuff," James stated bluntly.

"Uh, yeah," I moaned as I rubbed the events of yesterday out of my eyes. "I wasn't really planning on it, but it's become a pretty big part of me recently."

"You know these people haven't cared for you a single day before whatever it was happened to you?" James lashed out.

"Hey man, you can't take responsibility for things you have no control over. I've never even been near here before a week or two ago. I know these people aren't exactly everyone's favorites, but it's not about how others perceive you it's about your relationship with God." I looked up to see the threesome more confused than I ever had. Their eyes were like a small child's that had been told Santa wasn't real for the first time.

I began to become frustrated that they couldn't see the world as I did. The space between us felt like miles. There were no words that could explain the choices I had made or the person I had become.

Kyle paused, "I don't know who you are anymore, but we followed you here--- we might as well go in." He stood abruptly and strode inside. My eyes followed, then looked back at the other two who shrugged and brushed past, leaving me on the steps. I looked up at the sky as if expecting to see someone or to get a pep talk.

Since neither happened, I sighed and walked in. Pastor Reynolds motioned me to the front pews. I told him of my journey finding what I wanted to say and what I had decided on. I sat by myself as the service began. My thumbs made imaginary circles around each other, afraid of contact but interested in the idea.

I had zoned out until Pastor Reynolds looked down at me for a moment and I realized I was being introduced. "It's easy to get in a habitual cycle or pattern," he explained, "but sometimes I find that I'm not the only one with something to say. Yet, I also find that everyone has something to say, some just need a place to say it. Today my friend Eron Basque is going to deliver us his story. Although we have just begun our journey together, something tells me there is more to this man than I know. I believe the Lord worked through him in worship last week, and I'm excited for how He moves in this young man today. So, without any further delay, please welcome Eron."

The congregation joined in an applause as I stepped on the platform. The pastor shook my hand and placed the other on my shoulder to show support. I shimmied behind the microphone and gazed out upon the crowd. As I began to reach for my notes, the front door of the church opened, and two people attempted to creep into the back rows. Thomas noticed that I saw him, and stopped abruptly, making eye contact with me allowing him to see my horror and surprise at the fact that the other person sneaking behind him was Amber.

I snapped back quickly, remembering what I was doing. A smile flashed across my face apologetically. My hand reached inside my jacket and came out empty. *"When James and Melanie brushed past me, the notes must've fallen out,"* I thought. I began to panic. The congregation shifted uncomfortably as they were now aware something was wrong. Everything I had wanted to say had been perfectly worded and constructed. I looked down at Pastor Reynolds. While everyone else stared at me confused, he remained confident. I couldn't let him down. I had already done that to too many people.

"When I was born I was told I wasn't exactly like other kids. My family started out with a normal life. We weren't rich by any means, but we got by. Yet, friends were a concept I wasn't familiar with. I started school but lived in another world while I was there. I spent my days drawing, imagining, and learning guitar from my dad. As a kid, I never asked what my dad did. I never knew he had lost his job a week before I was born. I never knew what he did to take care of me. I never knew he was a drug dealer."

The crowd stopped whatever they were doing at the word. This had caught their full attention, yet for me it was just a part of my past. I wasn't trying to go off of a paper, I was just telling my story.

"Although for me, that didn't mean much. I lived in my own fantasy. I didn't play sports. I didn't have friends. I was caught up in a world of my own and I never imagined it would end. But my dad's business made sure it did."

I paused. I was entering the part of my life no one knew about. Not one soul had heard these words, but slowly I proceeded. "I didn't expect our life to change. I didn't expect a man with a shotgun to end the life of both of my parents."

The congregation was dead silent. The only sound was my breath shaking. "The sound of that gun firing, the sound of my parents' screams, those are things I got past. The images that appear every time I close my eyes are what started the downhill spiral. The man that took their lives dragged me out of the house, and who my father really was began to come into the light."

"The next few years were some of the most impactful as I was old enough to understand but not old enough to do anything about where I was. From the time I was eight until I was sixteen, I spent my time in old warehouses, meeting hundreds of people but never learning their names, and selling whatever came into my possession in order to stay alive. I didn't have friends before my parents died, and I didn't exactly find many after. I sat by and watched the rest of the world carry on, as if my section of life didn't exist to them."

"I was successful in what I did though. I began receiving other assignments that offered greater pay. Yes, I needed the money, but I was asked to commit acts of violence I couldn't commit. So, as you might say, I faked it till I made it. I found another solution to every task in order to prevent death or damage. I was living a lie on multiple levels. But as I began to deteriorate mentally from this deceit and grief I found a group of friends that looked out for me. I didn't know what that was like. I didn't know what I had." I made eye contact with Kyle, James, and Melanie. Their eyes stared like a person waiting for a picture, believing if they blink they'll miss it.

"They were my sanity. In a world where falling short was a habit, they insisted I was enough. I just wish I had believed them. As with every lie though, it must come to an end. There must be a revelation. It was a suspenseful night in August and a conflict between our gang and a rival gang had reached its climax. My boss's life was in danger, and it was up to me to save him. It was up to me to pull the trigger and kill the man who held him at bay. I couldn't do it. I dropped the gun. My boss looked at me and swore if he made it out alive he'd kill me. So I ran. I ran from him, from the business, from my past, from my pain, from my friends, from everything." My head fell as I wasn't sure how to formulate indescribable feelings.

"I hated myself. I tried to find worth in my life and found nothing. I slept during the days and snuck around at night, hoping not to encounter anyone or anything. I scavenged for food when I needed it, and made do with minimal shelter. I was unable to look forward. Every thought that went through my mind made me hate myself more. I found pleasure in destroying myself. I was dying from the inside out. There was a small slice of me that wanted to live, but it was always darkened by the rest of me. I'm not doing a great job right now capturing the feelings that were so prevalent in my life." I paused.

"It's like failing to breathe. Not because you can't but because you don't believe you deserve to. It's a brand-new car with a broken engine. It's like you're drowning, while everyone else is swimming around easily. I'm still new at this Bible stuff, but it's like Adam. A man that had the potential to be something and to live but was a screw-up that failed to fulfill his purpose. That's me. I was hoping maybe I could make God's job easier and just take a pest out of this world. After four months of living like this, I had made up my mind. I found a fire escape and threw myself off of it. I wanted to end it all. Somehow, I survived though. A gracious man and his daughter took me in."

For some reason this was the section of my story that I

began to get emotional about. I guess the emotions had never really been dealt with and there was a lot of rawness to feel.

"They gave me a new life. I began a new school, I participated in athletics, I was a new Eron. More specifically the daughter showed me I could be a new Eron. She cared about me regardless of everything. She encouraged me to pick up music again. She saw what I didn't. I loved her for that. But if there's any advice I could give you it would be: don't run. Running feels good while you're doing it, but when you stop, everything that was troubling you before is still there, waiting for you I had become absorbed in my new life. I still didn't know about God, but I found Him to be present in my life for the first time."

"Now the man's daughter. I said I loved her. This past week I've been looking into what that means. I looked to how Jesus described it. I have a long way to go, but I think I'm starting to get the idea. And now I can say, for the first time in my life and without doubt, I truly love her. Not in the love that we use to describe our hobbies or good food. The kind of love that's given at a wedding. The love that conquers death and anything the world could produce. The kind of love that isn't an emotion, but a commitment, one that I still want to keep. I think a lot about why she was introduced into my life. I may never know that answer. But I feel like God gave her to me not because I had anything to give, but to show me there were things to live for."

It was interesting. At this point, the congregation began to change. They began to realize that although our experiences had been different, the way we felt because of them was not.

"Yet, as I've learned, everything in this world is temporary. As I returned from prom with this girl, there inside the house was the man I had left to die in the warehouse from the gang months ago, with a gun to her father's head. Once again, I did the only thing I had ever done or knew to do – I ran away. My life had returned to square one. It was in this moment of despair, this moment of pain, that I fell at the steps of this building and that's where Pastor Reynolds found me. Like I said, I didn't think much of my life. The moments in my new life were some of the best, but in the end, they led me to the same place. But God saw something I didn't: potential. In the end, I broke on this floor and gave my life to Christ. Since then, I've changed, but my life really hasn't. The love I once treasured in my life isn't reciprocated. The self-hatred that has become a part of my blood is still a present in my life. I don't have a family or place to stay. And I've left a lot of people behind, and that I regret.

But there's one thing that I have now that's stronger than all of that, something God's given me: hope.

I don't feel qualified to stand before you all and teach, but I think I'm starting to comprehend what hope is. It's more than just guessing the cards on the table and thinking it may possibly go your way, it's knowing that whatever the cards are, the outcome of the game will still be in your favor. Hope is everything when you have nothing. Honestly, it's all I have, but it's enough. While God is still around, there is possibility."

I paused. I realized that I had no subject, idea, or central thought to this talk. I didn't even have a Bible verse to refer to. But this was me being vulnerable.

"I don't have anything from the Bible to back up what I said. But let my life be an example of what God can do and who He is. Because if I could be confident about one thing, it would be: the fact that I am alive means God is alive. I don't know what tomorrow will bring. I know a lot of what I've told you is probably worrying everyone more than it is helping. But as uncertain as everything is," I paused, "I can't wait to find out."

I looked around the church unsure of what to do next. I slowly made my way to the back of the church. After the first step everyone began applauding. After a few seconds I realized that they were applauding me. I looked down at my feet uncomfortably and continued walking. I almost reached the back door but hit a body before I did. My head looked up to see Thomas smiling at me.

"I thought I knew you man, but I had no idea," he commented. Melanie, James, and Kyle made their way behind me.

"Hey man, I still don't understand it, but that's something I don't think I could ever do. And, as much as I thought it was stupid, crazy, and insane... that was really cool," James said smiling, extending his hand. I returned the gesture and brought him in for a hug.

"Who are these guys?" Thomas asked.

"Oh, these are old friend-," I corrected myself, "This was my family when I had none, I owe them everything. This is James, Kyle, Melanie. Guys, this is Thomas, he was one of my first friends at the school I attend now, and he---- wait why are you here?"

"Oh yeah! Although I don't know you as well as these guys obviously, I could tell something was up with you. I have a friend that's pretty involved here that said you played a little while back and thought I'd come check it out. And I also brought a friend with me," he explained as he motioned to a familiar female face.

"Hey," I released from my body, like the last breath of a balloon.

Lanning

# CHAPTER EIGHT

"Hey." Amber did a quick sweep of the room with her eyes and then came back to me. "When did all *this* happen?"

I looked at her with a sheepish smile. "Wanna go for a walk?"

She nodded quickly and I thanked my friends for coming, promising I would catch up with them as well. This time I meant it. I began to walk out of the church when Pastor Reynolds called from behind me. "Eron!" He bellowed.

He grabbed my shoulder tenderly and extended his hand. "That wasn't exactly a conventional sermon, but I think that was one of the best talks that's been given. It was what a lot of people needed to hear. And I think one of the biggest testaments of who God is, and definitely one of the most impactful, is our testimonies. This is just the beginning for you my friend. I think you'll find things will work themselves out in a funny way. And as for what's going on right now I'd love to become a greater part of your life. Lunch sometime this week?"

I thought for a moment. What he was offering wasn't a replacement of my father, or a new friend. It was something unique. He wanted to be a part of my life in the way that a stake allows the vine of a plant to climb on it, guiding it to a new height and bringing about stability.

"Yeah, yeah I'd love that." I returned his handshake and left the church with Amber. Walking down the steps I glanced over my shoulder at the letters on the entryway: First Baptist Titchadesh. The city that had held so much and had so much left still. I exhaled through my nose in a small chuckle at it all.

As Amber and I began to walk down the sidewalks I caught her up on recent events and things I hadn't been quite honest about. I told her about my brief athletic experience and my real feelings about being in the program and why I quit. Looking back, there had been more to that decision than I had realized. She asked questions about parts of my testimony and for the first time I didn't hold back. I told of Melanie, Kyle, and James and the history and reunion. While recounting just the past week I felt like I was speaking on years and years of memories. It's funny how time does that.

We walked until we stood at her doorstep. She looked at me as if to wrap up our time and thoughts, but I knew there was something I had to do. "Is your dad home?" I asked. She looked at me horrified. I tried to be confident but my insides felt what her face portrayed. "I need to do this."

I walked up to the door, knocking with no confidence in my abilities, but praying that God would keep carrying me through. I saw Jack appear in the glass frame and barely recognized him. The confidence was still there, but it was behind a disfigured face. His cheeks were littered with welts and stitches. He was cleanly shaven revealing a bruised jawline. He opened the door abruptly. Amber stood in the drive near the road. "Mr. Bentwell can I talk to you?" He nodded in silence and motioned for me to come in.

I sat on the sofa as he placed himself in his recliner, waiting on what I had to say, but doubting it would change the thoughts in his head. His hands tapped on the armrests, multiple fingers covered in shades of purple and red with one in a splint. "I-I'm not sure where to start. But, it's information that's no longer mine to withhold."

I began telling him the story that I had told three times today. It had begun to be exhausting, but also comfortable. This story was mine. It was my life, and no one could take that from me. His reaction remained unwavered throughout all of it, which surprised me, but I continued until I had caught up to the night of prom.

"So, I ran. I ran like the coward I am. I put you and your daughter in danger after all you gave me. I don't expect you to forgive me or to even talk to me, but I had to try. I'm done living in fear."

He said nothing for a while, sizing me up. "Thank you for telling me this. I appreciate that. As for what occurred the other night, however, I can't have that happening to my family. I'm sorry son, this is the end of my generosity. I'm happy you found hope, but I don't believe in all of that. I don't know about Jesus Christ, or salvation, or whatever, but I do know I have responsibility with this family and that's my priority. You're welcome to grab the clothes and items we gave you during your time, but after that please leave my home."

I sighed heavily. I deserved the treatment I was receiving. It was hard news to take in, yet it was my decisions that had brought me to that point. I got up and began to make my way to the stairs.

"Oh, and Eron," Jack interjected. I looked back at him. "I know you and my daughter are close, and with you both being in school you two will encounter each other, but other than that I want you to stay away from her, do you hear me?"

I swallowed the sting. "Yes Sir." I turned back around and made my way to my room before he could see the pain written across my face. I grabbed the clothes out of the closet and stuffed them in an old duffel bag. I walked over to the guitar, gently resting it in its case and placing all of my music inside the exterior pocket. I looked around the room in search of anything I forgot. My eyes rested on the old bureau. I hadn't opened it since I had arrived. Curious, I walked over and pulled the worn-down drawer out. Inside were three old photo albums. My hands grazed over the dusty covers. I picked up the middle album gingerly. The black exterior was laced with gold lining, yet there was no label identifying the contents. I opened the cover to see a photo with three people in it. The man on the right was clearly a younger Jack. He had slightly more hair and more of a youthful glow, but other than that he was the same man I had left downstairs. However, something was different. He seemed almost relaxed. He didn't look tense or stressed, but truly joyful.

The girl in the middle I assumed was Amber as a young girl. Her brown hair was shorter and curlier, but the eyes were the exact same, containing wisdom beyond years.

The woman on the left was new to me. Her skin was lighter than Jack and Amber's. Her figure was thin and fit. She seemed to be a woman that took care of herself well. Her face was strikingly beautiful and exactly like Amber's.

"I see you found mom."

I jumped in surprise. I began to cram the albums back into their drawer, knocking over everything. As it all shuffled, something caught my eye but I wasn't able to think about it as my mind was thinking rapidly of things to say.

"I guess we never really told you about that one did we," Amber concluded. "The truth is-"

"Amber get down here," Jack bellowed. "He needs to get going." She gave me a slight smile and exited. I turned back to the drawer. Under the albums that had been shuffled lay a Model 10 Smith & Wesson revolver. I looked around in confusion. There was no reason for a family in the suburbs of a nice city in a nice neighborhood to own such a powerful handgun. It hadn't been touched in years by the looks of it. I opened it to see one bullet in the chamber. I began to shuffle through the drawer some more. I finally found a pamphlet that had the woman from the photograph on the front. "Laurie Bentwell: February 21, 1967 - August 14, 2009." As the pieces of the puzzle began to fall into place I heard Jack's voice once more. "Eron you almost done up there?"

"Yes sir, coming right now," I yelled, tossing the gun into my bag and closing the drawer. I zipped up everything and grabbed my guitar and left the Bentwell's, travelling to some-where.

------------------------------------------------------------------------

The next few weeks were strange, yet oddly fulfilling. After our first lunch, Pastor Reynolds insisted I stay with him and his wife, Jordy, for the time being. I still attended school. Although no one knew of my situation other than Thomas and Amber, I felt very awkward. I was entering a new phase of my life and was unsure of how to properly conduct myself. I continued to branch out and gain confidence, not letting everyone in, but extending myself out a little more each day.

My afternoons were spent working at a job downtown that Pastor Reynolds had arranged or playing music. On the occasion I would meet with Melanie, James, and Kyle and work on re-establishing those relationships. Thomas continued to be a presence in my life. He was one that constantly surprised me. He had even begun to date Amber's friend, Tori. Yet he always made time for me and checked up on me. After everything, he deliberately chose to make me a part of his life.

The evenings were spent with Pastor Reynolds. He would pour wisdom into me, guide my readings, and diligently tend to my relationship with Christ. I had started to read the Bible, learn what it means to pray, and understand more and more of the

God that yanked me out of my life for some purpose.

It was a very odd and constantly evolving time in my life, but I found a large sense of security in it.

There was stress and worry though. Graduation was getting closer and closer as May was coming to a close. I was on schedule to graduate as my testing had gone well, but I hadn't applied to college anywhere and no idea how to do it or where to apply. I definitely couldn't afford it yet. I had just put it off until it was a necessity. Time just kept going on by.

Through it all, I still thought about Amber. We didn't really communicate anymore, which broke me. Every night she was in my prayers. Almost every song I wrote was in some way about her. Her memory weighed heavily upon me, but I was still unwilling to let it go. It became easier as I grew closer to Christ, but the burden was still clinging powerfully.

Nonetheless time waited for nothing and May 25th came. I sat in the crowd of students watching those that had succeeded give speeches of their experiences until I got up to cross the stage myself and receive a piece of paper that held no real meaning for me. The last student received her diploma, and before I knew it hats were flying in the air as high school had reached its end.

I left the central area and found Pastor Reynolds and his wife. "Proud of you Eron. Never thought you'd be here did you?" He asked.

I laughed. "Not in a million years."

I found Thomas and expressed my congratulations. I thought about finding Amber but came to the conclusion that it wasn't my place. Most of the students headed out to attend a post-graduation party, but I knew I had some thinking to do instead.

I told Pastor Reynolds where I was headed and began walking. The beginning of summer had hit and the warm air felt comforting. After traveling a mile or two I arrived at my destination. My eyes looked over the lake. Except this time, it wasn't from a cliff. I had spent so long looking from afar and I felt now was the time to experience Lake Timor up close. I traveled along the bank, taking it in, when I saw an old dinghy washed up on the shore. Gingerly I turned the boat over. There didn't seem to be any holes, just an old fishing net and a double-sided oar. I drug the boat over to the nearest dock and boarded the boat, shoving off into the waters. The waters contained not one ripple as I lay in the boat staring up at the stars.

*I wonder what's next? Fifteen years from now where will I be?* As those thoughts brought about more worry than I realized, I quickly shut them down and simply existed. My mind cleared of everything. The water settled any adrenaline and the clouds moved slowly above.

It was weird. My whole life, I had constantly looked for peace. Often it seemed that peace was the most important thing. But now that it was given to me I wasn't sure I could handle it. Peace is often associated with silence. Silence eliminates distractions. When distractions are eliminated we are left with just ourselves. That's a terrifying thought. I fought this fear until my body allowed itself to just exist.

After about an hour of enjoying the evening it was getting late and I decided to head back. I didn't want to keep Pastor Reynolds and Jordy up waiting. I sat up and began to paddle back. I had drifted quite a ways, but as I got closer I thought I saw bright lights on the dock. I couldn't imagine anyone being out on the lake that late, but it was clearly a group of people. Then I noticed the blue and red lights in the background.

I paddled into the dock. "Sir, please exit the boat, keep your hands where we can see them." I looked around confused but followed their directions. The officers helped me up on the dock.

"What's going o-"

They flipped me around and handcuffed my wrists together. "Eron Basque, you are under arrest for previous sale and distribution of contraband, illegal ownership of firearms, assault, tax evasion, fraud, and attempted murder. Also, theft as I assume this boat isn't yours. We have warrant from the judge of Filotimo County based on sworn testimony and you are being taken into custody. You have the right to remain silent. Anything you say can and will be used against you in a court of law. You have the right to an attorney. If you cannot afford an attorney, one will be provided for you. Do you understand the rights I have just read to you?" The officer questioned. My mind flooded.

"Yes Sir."

"With these rights in mind, do you wish to speak to me?"

"Yes Sir. I-I mean I don't know what exactly to say as this is kind of a lot to take in at once. Who testified to all this?"

"Mr. Jack Bentwell, sir."

# CHAPTER NINE

Just as I began to process what was going on, I was being moved to another area, or questioned by another person. I didn't say much, since I didn't know what they knew, and I wasn't about to give them anything. By the questions they were asking and the detailed accusations, I had a feeling they knew a lot more than I would have wanted them to know. After pictures, fingerprints, and other standard procedures I was ushered into a temporary holding cell and told further questioning would take place in the morning.

I expected my thoughts to keep me up, but I found myself empty and unraveled on the suspended bed.

My eyes opened to rattling on the barred door. The officer from the previous evening barked at me to get up and follow him. He asked tensely who I would like to contact. When I said Pastor Reynolds from First Baptist Titchadesh his expression portrayed complete confusion. He led me to an almost empty room and told me he would return soon with either the Pastor or a message from him. The room contained a single table bolted into the ground. On the side by the door were two identical chairs. On the opposite side was a chair identical to the first two facing the door. The wall by the door held a large mirror, which I presumed was a one-way mirror for interrogation purposes but I had no way of proving it. With no other option I sat in the singular chair and looked into the mirror. It was a peculiar image. My body looked healthy. My face stern and composed. Even my hair didn't look unkempt. Last night felt like I had taken a ten-mile hike, yet to the outside world and even myself, I looked fine. I looked like a normal person you would see hanging out with his friends or doing homework. I wasn't that kid. I was a criminal.

I was a criminal; I was something every parent dreads their kid becoming. I was something society portrays as the dirt of the class system. I was the lowest of the low. Yesterday I stood as everyone else. Now I was the dust on their feet. I thought I had only been processing these thoughts for a few moments when the door opened.

Pastor Reynolds and Jordy walked in. I rose to embrace them both. However, the embrace was brief and unmeaningful as we all knew there were more important matters to attend to. I took my seat back as they sat opposite to me. The officer left, sending in a single guard to monitor our conversation and keep the environment safe.

Pastor Reynolds placed his hands on the table, exhaling deeply. "I was afraid this day would come. I had prayed and hoped it never would."

Mrs. Reynolds sat stern, offering support. In that moment I began to realize the true sacrifice this couple had willingly taken on. They gave up freedom, security, financial stability, time, and now were involved with a crime they had nothing to do with, all because of a love for me. The capacity of such a love astonished me. It became clear why Jack ostracized me from his house. A love this strong would do whatever it took to ensure that the other was safe, even if it meant hurting someone else. It meant placing another life into a higher importance than your own. That was the love of a father. Even my own father, although he had his shortcomings, gave his life in the end to protect me. It was a debt I couldn't repay, but it was time to try.

"I don't want you guys to have to go through more for me. I have an idea. It's foolish. It's crazy. But it's what I have to do. Because of people like you, I'm here today. I've been given so many chances I've lost count. I have a purpose, one I need to fulfill. Can you bring in the officers?"

Pastor Reynold's eyes widened. "I don't know exactly what you're talking about, but if it's anything like what I'm thinking, no, we'll find another route."

My mouth began to open, but before I could speak his wife interjected. "Honey," she spoke smoothly, rubbing his arm, "I'm not as involved in this as you have been. Personally, I have no idea what will happen next. Truthfully, neither do you. But there is a fire in his eyes. The last time I saw that fire was when you told me you were taking the job as senior pastor of First Baptist Titchadesh. I don't know what it is he's going to do, but he needs to do it."

She looked at her husband earnestly. He returned the gaze, then shifted to me. He had never had a son. I was the closest thing. We had founded a relationship on something bigger than ourselves and it showed clearly. And now he was sending me out to take on... well, actually I don't know what he thought I was going to do, but I don't think he was far off from the truth. He pursed his lips.

"The necklace I gave you," he began, "was once my father's. It was a token of strength and, at various times, was all he had. When I first told him I was turning down an opportunity to become the head of a major corporation to pursue ministry, I thought he would have been disappointed. Instead, the biggest grin came across his face. He got out of the recliner and stood to face me, removing the necklace." Pastor Reynolds stood up and grabbed my hands tenderly. "He placed the necklace in my palm and told me, 'Son, the two most important days of your life are the day you were born, and the day you learn why. It's always hard to let go of someone. But we're all a part of something greater than ourselves, and when God calls, the best thing we can do as fathers, is to tell you to pick up the phone. I'm proud of you.'"

I didn't know whether all of that was his father, or Pastor Reynolds's words, as every syllable was spoken with meaning and passion. His hands laid on mine, looking into my eyes, displaying satisfaction at who I had become. His wife smiled and exited to go get the officers.

He then did something I'd never forget. He knelt down at the feet of my chair and took off his shirt. He grabbed a water bottle from the tabletop and poured it onto the cloth. He then removed my sandals and began scrubbing my feet. As he did this, he started to pray over me. He prayed for strength. He prayed for courage. And rather than for victory or triumph, he prayed for God's will to be done in what came next. I heard the creak of a door but Pastor Reynolds continued, unfazed.

I looked up to see the officers enter. The first man immediately tried to run to the scene and break it up, but the officer from the previous night held him back, taking in the situation, mesmerized. The pastor's wife simply smiled in joy.

Pastor Reynolds finished washing my feet. He stood up

and looked me in the eyes. I met his gaze as we came to a point of closure.

"Thank you, for everything," I said.

He nodded. He turned to the officers. Pastor Reynolds was an older man, shirtless, in an interrogation room, but there was no shame about him. He addressed the officers. "Thank you, men. Jordy and I will be outside."

I strapped the sandals back on my feet and realigned my chair at the table. The two officers took a seat, still caught off guard by the scene they had intruded.

The officer from the previous night shifted uncomfortably. The man on the right now looked unsure, as the first officer seemed to be his superior. The first officer began to open his mouth, "Hello Mr. Basque, again I am Captain-"

I interjected. "Sir, I don't mean to interrupt, but I'll tell you everything. I have nothing to hide. I believe there is a way we can help each other."

The officer gave me a confused look. The captain, however, shifted forward, interested. "Go, on."

# CHAPTER TEN

My feet sliced quickly through the June afternoon. Although my body felt confident, my heart raced. Around me life was in full swing. Summer had kicked off, and with that, the atmosphere of the town was completely different. Things seemed more relaxed and life was easier.

This aura made me seem like the odd one out once again. But it was okay. I wasn't going to the beach. I wasn't making plans or socializing. I wasn't traveling. I was confronting one of the biggest fears of my life.

I reached the edge of downtown. The luxurious half of the city disappeared behind me. I continued through the older businesses. The letters faded on the walls, falling away to make room for the new. Trash began to litter the ground more and more. I made my way past these areas until I entered the slum-- the eyesores of Titchadesh. This was the region that most of the city tried to forget existed. This was where I grew up.

I walked through familiar streets: The houses where I had crashed on the sofas; the yards where I had encountered the best and worst of faces. The world that many looked at as a horror movie was my home. I didn't feel the danger most people assumed was lurking here. To me, these were just places that held real people with dreams, desires, and wishes. They had the same right to happiness as anyone else. I finally reached the end of the neighborhoods and came to a place that intersected with the river. I turned left and walked by the water for some distance. I didn't stop to think about the distance I had walked as it was the least of my worries. As it is with most major occasions, thousands of thoughts filled my mind of how things would go. There were a million different sentences I could formulate. I could play the situation with many intents. My mind whirred with the possibilities.

I finally reached the warehouse complex and stopped in front. I hadn't been inside this place in over a year. So much had happened.

I took a deep breath. I entered the fenced courtyard and after less than ten steps a voice resounded, "stop." I turned to face two men with rifles pointed at me, my hands rose in the sky.

"Eron Basque, I'm here to see Cameron." The men looked at me quizzically. It didn't seem that my introduction had made an impact on the men. I sighed.

"The Project," I tried introducing myself again. One man continued to point the gun at me, but the other's eyes widened and he lowered his weapon.

"The Project. Now that's a name I haven't heard in a while," the gruff man uttered. "How do I know it's really you?"

I slowly lowered down into a squat and pulled up my pant leg to reveal yet another secret in my life. On my right ankle, two Chinese symbols were tattooed into my skin. The first to show affiliation with the gang, the second was the same as my father's.

The man nodded. "Is he expecting you?"

"No, but I think me being here is going to be something he wants to address himself." The man squinted in the sunlight and nodded his head.

"Pete go send word to the boss, I'll watch over our visitor," he commanded the other man. Pete acknowledged the order and walked off into the compound. The first man walked up to me and began to pat me down. He grabbed the phone from my pocket and held it in front of me.

"C'mon, Proj, you should know better than to have this on you." I shrugged my shoulders as he stowed the phone away. "Why is it you came back anyway, you were free weren't ya?" He stopped patting me down "You don't remember me do ya? The name's Victor. I guess everyone just knew you as The Project. Cam's little project," he laughed. "But I don't think even that's gonna save you from what's gonna happen. Cam's little project almost gets him killed then runs off only to come back. He's gonna make you pay for that. You shoulda stayed disappeared."

I looked at Victor intensely. I honestly didn't remember him, but then again, I didn't remember most of the people here.

I didn't think anyone even knew who I was other than Cameron. "Guess I didn't think anyone paid attention to me. But freedom is relative I guess. Yeah, I was walking around out there, but Lord knows I was still enslaved. Am enslaved."

Victor chuckled. "Strong words. You think we're slaves? I mean, sure things ain't perfect, but here we have a sense of belonging. Ole Cam offers us security and a place to be, that's somethin."

I remained silent, keeping his gaze. It was sad because I had felt the same way at one time. It's always hard to see outside a storm when you're in the middle of it. I remembered seeing something on the news a few weeks back of a local girl that was in a violent relationship and was killed by her boyfriend. Her friends always spoke of how they saw it and had tried to get her to leave him before he seriously hurt her, but she never did. She was so consumed in her desire to be loved and to have someone, that she was blind to the fact that he was destructive. It's so often that we have a space in our life that needs to be filled. Therefore, when something comes along that we think might fit, we shove it in that space, even if it's not right. We're so desperate for these things that we fall in love with ideas and desires and become blinded to their reality.

That's when it hit me. Was it possible, that all this time I was only in love with the idea of Amber? All the time I spent with her, I had been so desperate for love and to have someone in my life. Desperation is a dangerous game.

"Hey man, you good?" Victor asked. I realized I had gotten enveloped in my thoughts.

"Well, well, well! I did not expect to see this," Cameron bellowed from the front doors. He strode slowly up to me. "Eron Basque, it is a pleasure!" He shook my hand firmly. His eyes burrowed into mine, searching for a clue or indication as to my reason for coming. "Now, I just want to recap here and make sure I have my story straight."

Cameron folded his hands in front of him and pursed his lips as though considering. He continued, "Now, when a source of labor goes missing or breaks, a new one is needed. That's business. Therefore, when your dad couldn't produce, we brought you in. I had to raise you a little, that's true. You were a kid. Rather than get rid of you, I give you a job and a place to be. You become difficult. I keep you around. I don't do that for most people do I, Victor?"

"No sir, you do not."

"Precisely. But, for you, Eron, I make an exception. Next thing you know, a couple errors occur and tensions get high. We get involved in some real-"

I interjected, "Then I disappoint you and everyone here with my inability to go through with anything, letting you down. Then I leave and run from everything multiple times. Even being here shows a lot of audacity. What could I possibly be coming to you about?" I paused to let the question sink in. "I've made mistakes. I know. I've messed up. I let you down. But it's worse out there than it is here. The world out there doesn't care, but you did. I'm here to ask for your forgiveness if you'd ever consider taking me in again."

Cameron sat back, perplexed. "Well, I'll be damned. Nemo finally learned the aquarium ain't where he wants to go. You forget Eron, I used to be in that tank. I had a nice house. I had a nice car. I even had a wife and my own business. But you know what? The world doesn't care about what makes you happy. The world wants to see you fail. The world would rather see you lose your business, your job, your house and car. The world doesn't give a damn if your wife leaves you! So you find your ways to give the world back the grief it gave you."

Cameron's voice had grown louder the more he talked, laced with a bitter venom toward all he had lost. After a moment, he continued, this time in a softer, more instructional tone.

"You forget that I'm not here because this was my top choice at graduation. I'm here because if the world's going to try to label me a criminal, then a criminal I'll be. And a damn successful one I've become. And hey, if I gotta shoot a couple guns, intimidate some bums, or add some items to my conscience to stay on top, so be it. This is who I am. This is who you are too."

He sighed and strolled up to me. "Boys, leave me and Eron alone for a minute." Pete and Victor returned back to their posts. Cameron got close to me and looked me dead in the eyes. I had spent many days running from a moment like this. There was nothing left but a hope that there was forgiveness somewhere in a cold man.

"Now, listen. Yes, you were different than most. You know that. But I have a business to run here. I'd let you come back, but what kind of example would that be to these kind folks that have been loyal to me? What kind of *lesson* would you be receiving if everything simply returned to how it was?" Cameron paused to let the question sink in. He seemed to be considering his next move as if he didn't know what he was capable of. He continued, "Am I glad to have you back? Yes. But, you are going to start at the very bottom. We're going to see if you really have changed. From now on, you don't go anywhere without my say so. You will be by my side twenty-four seven and will complete anything and everything I need you to. And guess what? Your assignments will start with the things you would never do."

My heart dropped. I wanted back in, but there was no way I could continue with it if this was my assignment.

I nodded my head. "Yes sir."

He returned the gesture approvingly. "Yes sir is right. Oh, and if you act up again, there will be metal between your eyes. It's nothing personal, just business. Now, my boy Pete was about to go out and make some deliveries. Go with him. I need you back in the swing of things."

"Yes sir," I muttered. I turned away from him and exhaled deeply.

"Eron where in the world did you get that watch?" Cameron called after me. I looked down at the black and grey G-shock on my wrist, a high-end watch for someone who had been on the streets.

"It was a gift from that man you held the gun to when you saw me that night," I lied.

"Hmm," he pursed his lips and fell silent, accepting my answer. I continued on towards Pete and we walked towards the exit of the compound together.

"Better get your accuracy up Eron," Cameron yelled after me.

He turned to shout to some at the entrance of the building, "It looks like we got ourselves a new hitman!"

------------------------------------------------------------

The next few hours were all too familiar. Nightfall was upon us as we went around town making deals. I had done this so many times before that now it was like simple muscle memory. The difference was that now these deliveries were littered with guilt. My only consolation was that it was for a greater good.

After a few deals, Pete broke off to meet someone at a shopping center. I was sent into the downtown strip. I was trudging down the sidewalk when I heard a familiar voice behind me.

"Eron?"

I continued walking.

"Eron, hold on." Amber's hand grabbed my shoulder and whisked me to face her. "Hey I know we can't exactly talk but-"

I flipped back around and continued walking, ignoring her. I had to get my deliveries done soon or questions would be asked. Plus, I wasn't exactly in the place where I wanted to talk to her. Well, I guess I did. I just couldn't without jeopardizing both of us.

"Okay, if you don't want to talk to me that's fine, but you don't have to be like this. I'm still a person!" She yelled after me. I gritted my teeth. The longer this went on, the more attention it would draw. I had to end the conversation quickly.

"So am I! But that didn't stop your dad from having me arrested!" Her eyes widened in surprise.

"Oh, he didn't tell you that? Yeah, he had me arrested. Told the authorities everything I've ever done. Now-" I stopped myself. "I can't even tell you what I'm doing right now."

She stood back in shock. "What do you mean you can't tell me? I thought you just left! I deserve to know what's going on, especially if my dad... what did you-"

"I just can't! Why do you care anyway? I thought you wanted nothing to do with me anymore? Let's keep it that way."

I turned and sprinted off, not waiting to hear her response. I didn't know where that anger came from but it scared me. So many emotions were built up, the smallest nudge would tip the whole balance over. I don't know if my actions were justified, but my emotions were too powerful to logically act. I cut into an alley to lose her if she tried to follow. As I exited the alleyway and came to another street, a blue Chevy Impala pulled up in front of me and rolled down the window. The officer from the interrogation room sat at the wheel. "Get in for a moment, son."

I looked around before entering the vehicle.

"Look, I understand you're going to see people you know. These people need to be avoided. Or at least refrain from making a scene. We can't afford to have this blow up, or we could both be screwed. Okay?"

"Understood," I replied. "How long do I have to do this, they are wanting to use me to take other people out."

"We heard. We just need you to report on the kind of

ammunition and manpower they have. It's the only thing stopping us from putting together a team to take Cameron out. He's made serious threats, and we have to determine the credibility of these threats. If we can discover evidence that Cameron has the capabilities to pull off what he's said he's going to do... well then, it's going to take more force than our local unit is capable of to take him down."

He continued, "Once you can get us that information, in addition to your recordings of his confessions, we'll have enough to put him behind bars."

He looked at me and attempted a smile. "But hey," he said, "the hard part is done. You're in. That's the farthest anyone has gotten so far. Our past spies didn't even make it through the door. It was too suspicious. So, well done on that."

I smiled sheepishly. "Yeah." I began to exit the vehicle. "You have the fake stuff, right?"

He nodded. He handed me various amounts fake contraband. This had been a condition of our deal. I knew once Cameron found out it I was giving out fake stuff, it would be game over. But for the sake of my conscience, I had to. I handed over the real stuff to him and left the car.

--------------------------------------------------------------------------

After the last delivery, we finally returned to the compound. I walked up to Cameron's quarters and checked in. Realizing the small amount of time at hand, I asked Cameron if I could find myself a weapon for future tasks. He was taken aback, but overjoyed at my eagerness. He sent me down to the armory to find something that I would feel comfortable with.

I entered the large room and was met by a slender, middle-aged woman. Her dark hair was laced with silver, and her face was marked by aging lines. It was obvious she was no longer in her prime.

"You must be The Project," she said, as I approached. "The name's Mack." She seemed as if at one time she would've greeted me with a hug or tried to find out more about me, but she no longer had the energy or desire. She was a shell of what she once was. Then again, so were many of the people that remained here.

She almost looked familiar, like I had seen her before, though I couldn't think of when. I dismissed the notion and cast my gaze around the room. I still hoped as I continued looking for a gun that maybe a memory or something would present itself

"So," she went on routinely, "we don't have a big array of long-range rifles because those are hard to come by. I'd imagine he just wants you to get a revolver, or maybe a pistol with a suppressor. Any preference?"

As she spoke, a hunch began forming in my mind. I tried to dismiss the thought as it arrived, but it lingered. It didn't make sense. *Eron this is idiotic. You know what you saw,* I told myself.

Nonetheless I found myself saying, "How about a Model 10 Smith & Wesson."

Her eyes squinted at me, sizing me up. "That's an oddly specific model. Why such an old gun?"

She played it off well, but I knew I was on the right track and had to continue.

"I had a friend that once owned one. It was nice and had a lot of sentimental meaning to him. His name was Jack Bentwell. He was an interesting guy."

At the mention of Jack, her eyes betrayed what she was working so hard to hide from me. I almost didn't believe it, but my hunch was right.

"Hello Laurie."

# CHAPTER ELEVEN

"Who are you?" She exclaimed, taking a step back. "I think you have the wrong woman."

"No, I think I know who I'm talking to, but as to why you're here I have no idea." She looked around terrified. From the expression on her face, I guessed that a mental battle had begun to rage. She finally came to a conclusion and walked purposefully to the door, closing and locking the exit.

"How do you know what you know? What do you know?"

"My name isn't The Project. It's Eron. I had... an accident, and your husband and daughter took me in for a while. While I was there I found some old pictures, the pistol, and a funeral program. A funeral program for you. My relationship with your family was a unique one to say the least. Now, please fill me in."

She sized me up. "No, I can't. I'm sorry."

"You faked your death. Someone wanted you dead..."

That's when a recently discovered truth popped into my thoughts. Love wasn't a word that popped up in conversation. Love was a sacrificial commitment. It was the love Christ showed people. The love so strong it led Christ to give us His life willingly for the ones He loved. The conversation I had with Jack re-entered my mind.

*"If you want something bad enough, you'll do whatever it takes to get it, without question," he had said.*

"Someone wanted Jack, but... you went in his place."

She looked into me sorrowfully. It was no longer a choice of whether or not to share herself with me, it was the human need to empty herself. She had been living in the world as someone other than herself and she was exhausted. Words began to flow out of her mouth like a pipe that had been rusted.

She sat down on a bench in front of the counter. I lowered my body to the base of the end of one of the aisle shelves and looked up at her eagerly.

"Okay, none of this goes anywhere." She took a deep breath, looking around once again. "Jack, Cameron, and I went to high school together here in Titchadesh. Class of '85."

Taking a deep breath, she continued, "Jack and I were high school sweethearts, but Frank, or Cameron as he's known now, was Jack's best friend. They both went to college here in town and majored in Entrepreneurship. They often worked together on many projects. But shortly after college they bought out a local business, built it up, and then sold it for a profit. They continued to buy out businesses and sell them for a few years. They had a natural talent for it, and the money was rolling in.

Jack and Frank became wealthy. Jack bought the house that I assume he's still in now in a nice, high-end neighborhood. I was pregnant with Amber and was enjoying just being a housewife and pursuing my interests. Jack made enough for both of us. He had built a reputation for his accomplishments and was living the life every American man dreams of. Yet, he was still unhappy. He couldn't become satisfied in his constant pursuit of more.

This is where he began to get reckless with his money. He donated tons to charity, hoping some philanthropy would do him well. He splurged on vacations and luxurious items. He still didn't receive any fulfillment. He went through all our savings searching the Earth for what he wanted. He never found it.

Meanwhile, I was raising Amber alone. I didn't like who he had become, but I loved him. So, I stayed and waited for him to figure it out.

During these ventures, the businesses he had invested in started to plummet. I don't know if it was bad investing, the crash of the market, or simply bad luck, but he began to lose it all. He needed an out. He became hostile. Now, Frank had spent some money on an average house and a few things, but Frank had enough in his savings to keep himself afloat. Nonetheless, the two men were becoming desperate as their life's work was failing.

Then, two months later, Jack returned from a business trip to Mexico. He said he found out how to save it all. He never would tell me how that was.

But, things got better, so I didn't question it. Everything did improve. Life resumed as it normally did. That is, until the police showed up at our door. They said one of the employees turned in some messages and files to the P.D. and there were reports of Jack's business dealing with cartels along the Mexican border. They had been sending down money as an investment into an illegal business. There were mailings, recordings, and files all proving the exchange. Jack turned to face me. I was sitting on the sofa holding little Amber, unaware of what was going on. Jack sighed and invited the officers in to sit down. He gave them cups of coffee, and then proceeded to tell them all about his hunches of Frank's dealing with the cartel due to his recent near-bankruptcy.

The men nodded. They asked more questions. They thanked him for his time, then left.

Naturally I didn't know any better. I was shocked to hear of Frank's dealings, but I thought my life would resume as planned. For years my life was normal. I had forgotten the incident had ever happened. You see, Jack won the trial. Frank went to prison for years. Everything just kind of worked itself out.

Then, one night I was home alone reading. Jack had taken Amber out to get materials for a last-minute school project. I heard a knock on the door. I don't know who I expected at that hour, but to see Frank at the front door was one of the biggest shocks of my life. The second biggest shock was what he told me he learned.

While he was in prison he had done some investigating. Frank knew he was innocent and wanted to know what was going on. He took the information from the lawyers and trials and began to ask around the prison to learn more about the cartel he was accused of dealing with. It was only a matter of time before he found someone who had dealt with them. He learned that the same group had connections to Titchadesh and other cities in the south. It wasn't just a group, but an empire.

So, Frank spent his time behind bars. He became consumed with the culture that was around him. It's funny how much other people can influence you. Just who you surround yourself with can change who you are. Frank was a perfect example. As he told me this story, his eyes increasingly burned a fire within their depths. His words had venom in every syllable as he spat out every sentence. This was not the man I once knew.

He then explained that once he got out and completed his parole, he continued his investigation. He got in touch with the local group. It was there he found out the truth. Jack had been dealing with the cartel and had invested the company's money. It was Jack's crimes that Frank paid for. Frank wanted revenge."

Laurie began to cry shakily. I don't think that the story she was telling me had ever left her memories before that moment.

"What do you say?" she continued. "What do you say when you find out your husband is a criminal that's placed an innocent man behind bars to cover up his own shame? Jack destroyed Frank's life. All that was left was a shell of what he once was. I wanted to make it right, I wanted to take it all away, but I didn't know how. I told him--I told him I would talk to Jack and he just laughed at me. The emotions in Frank had been built up for years. He wanted-"

She covered her face with her hand, almost as if she was trying to block the world out as she handled her own sorrow.

"He wanted to kill Jack."

Her cries had become a broken hiccup. She was struggling to speak. I swiveled my head to make sure no one was entering.

"I had to think quick. I couldn't let my husband die and I wasn't about to try to counsel the man-"

"So, you offered yourself instead," I interjected. I had begun to think that I had a slight grasp on what love was, but the actions Laurie took for her husband, I couldn't comprehend the selflessness.

She nodded. "But," she swallowed, "my death wouldn't be any better when I thought about Amber. So, I came up with a solution. I told Frank I would work for him for nothing. Jack would still be in pain thinking he lost me, Frank would get free labor, and there was a chance that one day I could reunite with my daughter. I've been here since."

"How come I never saw you when I worked here before?" I asked, wracking my memory.

"You might have. One of my conditions was that I wouldn't be out taking part in any activities out there. I would stay out of the way and do the grunt work. Cleaning, organizing, stocking, maintenance, that sort of thing. Tell me, how are my husband and daughter?"

I began to tell her about my experience with the Bentwell's the best I could. She smiled when I spoke of my interactions with Amber and when I gained Jack's approval. She missed the life she once had. When I mentioned the incident after prom she stopped me.

"He had a gun to Jack and didn't shoot..." she wavered. I hadn't thought about the fact until now. Cameron had every means to finish the job with Jack. Laurie had spoken about how he had changed but maybe there was hope inside of such a broken man.

I told her about the injuries I noticed at first sight when I returned to the house but she shook her head.

"Maybe, he's grown, or maybe, he cut a deal with Frank. I wouldn't think he would stop at anything," she said faltering as the sentence went on.

Things were already complicated but the situation seemed to continually deepen. I finished the story up until the moment I entered the room. It might not have been smart to explain my true reasons for being there, but if I were to truly let good win out, I had to have hope. To be honest, I wasn't sure who was good anymore. Even the men and women that were a part of Cameron's compound had good in them.

I remembered my days working here. I remembered when I left and how it felt to have absolutely nothing. I remembered how it felt to have people look at you and to feel a division bigger than the Grand Canyon between the two of you based on social status. I remembered what it was like to be a part of something where everyone recognized that you had feelings and dreams and took you in for who you were. The people in this place weren't evil, just misguided. I needed to figure out how to finish my job, live according to my faith, and stay alive.

The door clicked and I jumped to my feet. Cameron marched in the room and tossed me a pistol. "Why in the hell is this door locked?" He questioned angrily, eyeing Laurie.

"I was locking up to clean and check inventory. Your boy is the last one I was gonna help," Laurie answered calmly.

He looked at her and back to me suspiciously. He then pointed at the gun in my hands.

"There you are. Enough talk. Hope this one works because you're up. Don't try anything funny."

---------------------------------------------------------------------------

I sat on a park bench twiddling my thumbs. The pistol was tucked into my waistband. The sun laid down its rays and disappeared below the horizon. Cameron expected me to trail a man who would exit the building across the street at any minute. I was to follow him to a discreet location and take his life.

I couldn't go to Pastor Reynolds and jeopardize his life. I couldn't go back to the police. They already knew what was going on and expected me to complete my task, as per our agreement. I couldn't go to Amber – I had already pushed her away. Melanie, James, and Kyle had already escaped this life, so I would never bring them into it again. This time, it was just me and God against the world.

As these thoughts floated about, my target exited the building. I got up and began to walk across the street when a voice broke my concentration.

"What's up Eron!" Thomas yelled as he ran down the sidewalk toward me.

"Good Lord. I know like six people in the whole world and I'm running into all of them," I muttered. "Thomas now's not a good time," I explained, pushing him out of the way.

"Dude I haven't seen you since graduation, at least tell me what you're up to!"

"I'm really sorry man, I gotta go."

He looked at me frustrated. He stopped me in the middle of the street and turned me to face him. "Look I know you like taking life on by yourself and shoving everything down so far to where no one can find it. But what's the point if no one can share the experience with you? Look, I know you have a life and places to go, but do me a favor and give me call? If you care about someone you'll make time for them, ya feel?"

My eyes widened. I hugged him with everything in me and sprinted after the man yelling my thanks behind me.

My target was a man in his twenties, tall and lanky. He had curly brown hair and a slight goatee. His name was Jared Longview. And I knew exactly what I had to do.

He continued walking down the street in a white hoodie and dark jeans. Luckily, I knew this town better than he did. I ran down an adjacent street and through a park to cut him off. I sat in the alley by the sidewalk he was traveling. As he passed I cocked the pistol. He stopped in his tracks at the click. I pulled

his arm, yanking him into the alley.
 "Hello Jared."

Lanning

# CHAPTER TWELVE

Jared looked around for something to get him out of the situation. "Hey man I'm not gonna shoot you, just listen." I put the pistol back in my waistband and sat him down next to me. "I work for Cameron. I was sent here to take you out as a message to your boss, but that's not who I am. So consider this as a warning. Keep your head low and say nothing and both of our groups can experience peace a little longer. Got it?"

He nodded. I sighed and turned around to walk out into the street. "Won't you be punished for this if Cameron finds out? I know I would be," he called after me.

I turned back around. "I don't know you. But I know there's people that would miss you. There's people that love you. You may not be in a good place right now, I know I'm not. But you have a life. You have places to go and things to do. Hold onto that. You may not have much, but there's breath in your body. Where there's life there's possibility. When you care about someone, you make sacrifices."

I left Jared standing there and started the walk back to the compound. I smiled as I knew that my actions might hurt me, but it was what Christ would have done. It's what Thomas would've done.

However, I knew there would be wrath to face upon my return. I walked back in darkness, thoughts attempting to break the barrier I had placed. With everything happening, I hadn't had time to process the events that were taking place. In a way that rush provided a sense of bliss in my life. The minute it ended was the minute I would face emotions or fears.

I don't think it was necessarily me running from the problems, but me being swept away in them so that I wouldn't know what was happening until I was set down again. It's kind of like falling down a hill. While you're tumbling you don't realize what's going on and adrenaline takes over. It's not until you stop and look over yourself that you see the scrapes and wounds and realize how hurt you really are. But that's also the moment where you see where you need to heal.

I returned to the compound, walking directly up to Cameron's makeshift office and tossed the pistol on the table. "Mission accomplished."

Cameron looked up from his table of disarrayed items. "Really?" He asked disbelievingly. He leaned back in his worn leather chair. "How'd you do it?"

I pursed my lips and thought quickly. "Saw the direction he was walking and cut him off when he was walking between buildings. I didn't waste any time talking, just did it."

He shifted his weight forward, resting his elbows on the table in front of him. "Anyone see?"

I shook my head.

"You know kid. You are many great things. But you've never been a good liar."

I didn't waver as he had no proof other than a hunch. "Why would I lie?" I asked. Cameron grabbed the pistol and popped open the chamber. He tilted the gun and three bullets fell out and clattered on the wood.

"I know you far better than you think I do. I gave you this gun with three bullets to ensure the job was done. And I do believe there are three still here." He stood up and walked out from behind the table. I tensed up.

"Relax. I'm a guy trying to find his way like you. And I'll tell you something. Nine times out of ten people will disappoint you. I think you're on number nine right about now, which means next time my good faith will pay off."

I don't know what was more ironic: the fact that he didn't consider himself a ruthless murderer or that this man believed in me so whole-heartedly. Maybe he wasn't as much of a lost cause as people thought he was. Then again, I had seen him commit acts that I would do anything to forget.

"Believe it or not I figured you wouldn't do it. But you see, Jared worked for a bigger group, and guess what? That group is the exact same one that screwed me over. Or should I say, the one that you helped screw us over. In two days, we are going at 'em. Not just straight up. We don't have numbers for that. But they've done a good job of picking a location where police won't be and disturbances aren't a thing so we'll be free to be strategic. Here's the catch: You're our front runner. My boys will be distractions while you go for the head dog so to speak. You're gonna finish what you couldn't. If you don't though, so help me you're going to bring out the man that the world thinks I am. That is if you live past the other guys.

This world doesn't give people like you and me second chances, but here you are on chance number fifty-seven or whatever. Sadly, everything in this world has an expiration date, including a person's patience. Do me a favor Project, don't screw this up."

My face remained unchanged. "Where is this place, and if you need this guy killed so badly why send me?"

He laughed. "Wouldn't you like to know. You'd be surprised what goes on under the surface of things. To most middle class suburban families, life doesn't go beyond their office jobs and kids' sports games. It's amazing how easy it is to hide in plain sight. As for why you, if you pull this off, congrats, you're back in. If you don't, well, let's say your life here is somewhat expendable. Sounds brutal, but sometimes life drives you to do what you never thought you would," Cameron pulled out his pistol. He crept up to me and put the barrel underneath my chin and my jaw clenched. "None of us ever plan to be where we are kid." He lowered the gun and stuck it back in his belt.

I nodded my head. I actually agreed with certain things he said. I turned around and began to walk out.

"Oh, and Eron, don't ever lie to me again. I don't know how you view me, but I'm still a man that appreciates some honesty."

I met his gaze, and turned down the hall, thinking about what Cameron said. There was a part of me that wanted to please him, as crazy as it sounded. He was the closest thing I had to a father growing up and I wanted the approval.

I hated that about myself. I wanted to just rest in knowing that I was enough, but I found myself constantly wanting another person to give me some thumbs up or tell me that I did a good job. It was a temporary happiness, but I would do anything for it. Even if the other person didn't really care.

I walked downstairs and entered the armory and sat

down at the base of the shelf again. Laurie was standing at the counter sorting bullets, patiently waiting for me to speak.

"Do you ever, just, I don't know, feel like the battles we fight are always labeled as problems, but in reality, we just keep creating them because they give us a purpose?" I asked.

She laughed. "You say 'we,' but I know you mean 'I,' so you're gonna have to get a little more personal if I'm to understand."

"I mean, every time my depression returns, or when it was constant, it was a choice to feel that way. I wanted out, yet I got comfortable in my own sorrows. I chose to pursue Amber, and it created so many insecurities and worries. Yet, I kept choosing it. I chose to become a Christian. Now, I can't do anything the people around me tell me to because I serve a different master. Even now, I choose to stay here, even though this isn't where I want to be. All these problems are due to my decisions, yet I keep making them as some sort of entertainment to my life. Then I get caught up in my decisions and lose sight of everything around me. I become reckless. I go too far." I ran out of breath to the point where I forgot where I was even going with the sentence.

Laurie sat for a moment pondering her response. "I'm not going to tell you what to choose or how to live. I don't think I have that right. Plus, if I had it figured out I wouldn't be here right now. Here's what I do know: there is one 'source spot,' as I like to call it, in your life. When you look at a river, the water has to come from somewhere. Whatever it's being filled with is what's gonna be in the rivers. I played volleyball in high school. That sport was my life and I spent every day practicing. Then one day me and a group of my friends went to go play a fun game of basketball, and I couldn't catch a rebound. Every time the ball came off the rim I would swat it out of there like a volleyball, not because I was a bad basketball player, but because volleyball was my source spot and it was affecting everything else in my life." She stopped what she was doing and addressed me directly.

"My point is this: whatever you put in your source spot is going to dictate a lot of your life. No matter if it's depression, Amber, Jesus, this place, volleyball, or whatever. And if you pursue your thing wholeheartedly, you're gonna be a little reckless, but it doesn't matter because that's what you chose. It's a menu not a buffet, you gotta choose something. You may feel moments of regret or frustration with your choice, but in the end you gotta have faith that you chose the best thing. And so what if you go too far? You may not have had a prime education but I'm sure you know that in the first village ever some guy had to be willing to go too far in order to get somewhere new. Some explorers planned out their whole pursuit and still died or screwed up. But then if everyone stopped exploring out of fear, nothing would've been accomplished. People have to keep trying because that's what people do."

"What if my recklessness gets others hurt?" I asked.

"When you pursue something recklessly a lot of people will look at you like you're crazy and walk away. They won't want to be a part of it, and they won't get hurt. But there's some people that see that recklessness and it excites them. They want to be part of it. They may get hurt. But they chose the same risk you did. They chose to go with you, no matter what happens. Those people are special. Hold onto them."

I nodded. I had thoughts about my new assignment swimming around in my head. I didn't know why, but I knew I needed to talk to Laurie after leaving Cameron's room. I needed confirmation of my feelings, but after what she said, I didn't need any confirmation. I needed her to say yes. My heart began to stir like water reaching its boiling point. The words flowed right out of my mouth.

"Laurie," I spoke confidently. She perked up and stood ready. "I have a reckless idea. You might get hurt. I most likely will get hurt. But I can guarantee it will be worth it."

Lanning

# CHAPTER THIRTEEN

I hopped off the bike and looked at Victor. The day had come. I had ridden to the drop-off point and the rest was an on-foot excursion. The sun was just setting, the evening wind rustling my hair gently.

"You know what you're doing?" Victor asked.

"Do any of us?"

Victor chuckled nervously. "Good luck Proj, you'll need it." He backed up his bike a few feet then sped away, leaving me alone. I stood on the edge of downtown. Behind me lay a bridge. I had half an hour to station myself, then the rest of Cameron's men would be there to divert the other gang's attention long enough for me to carry out my job – or die trying.

Families and couples walked around downtown with no regard for the world around them, no clue that a whole different world surrounded their comfortable existence. I remembered getting the opportunity to see a Batman movie when I was younger. I remembered watching Bruce Wayne change into Batman and wondering how no one ever figured out it was him I wondered how an entire battle could take place and no one would notice. Now it made sense. Unless something was put right in front of people's eyes, they did not see it, let alone wonder about it.

I took one last look at the town and began to walk across the bridge. A man stood with his arm around a woman as they watched the sunset. A group of young boys were trying to climb the bridge without being noticed. I laughed at their anti-authority ambition. I walked a little further and saw a familiar girl leaning on the railing. My eyes widened. I didn't know what God was trying to say or do, but He was nothing less than persistent with it.

Amber was deep in thought as I walked and I planned to let her remain there. I widened my path and continued walking, knowing my goal.

My heart beat rapidly as I passed her. As I continued walking I began to hear footsteps come towards me. Amber was now beside me, walking with me. I waited for her to say something, but she never did. We exited the bridge and began to enter neighborhoods. She remained by my side. We left the occupied roads and began to enter undeveloped land. She continued walking. I knew I was getting close based on the directions Cameron had given me earlier in the day.

"Okay," I stopped walking, "You need to go back." Amber didn't reply. She just stood there. "Amber you don't understand what's going on. This has nothing to do with us or where we left things. What I'm about to do isn't safe. I can't have you here. I'm sorry," I explained.

She stood there. "I don't care if I get hurt. I don't care what you're doing. I'm going. I know you don't want me in your life. I know my dad didn't handle things how I wish he would have. I don't know what will happen long-term, but I know what I need to do today. Since I heard you speak of your faith, I've started to look into it. One thing that I've found helpful is the Lord's prayer. It says "give us our daily bread." I've thought a lot about that, just focusing on what I need for today. Today, and every day before today, I've needed you."

I was already listening. But now I wasn't just hearing her words, I was feeling them. She wasn't speaking off of a plan, she was speaking from something greater than any plan.

"Nothing about change is easy. You and I both know that. But, I'm sick of trying to keep up with it myself. Am I angry at my dad? Yes. Am I angry at you? You better believe I am. Am I beyond confused about what's going on? Yes. But I'm done trying to find all the answers. I think it's time to enjoy the questions."

She grabbed my hand tenderly and spoke with the utmost sincerity.

"God... God spoke to me Eron. He told me to come to this bridge. I've been here for half an hour. I got frustrated and prayed that God would tell me what to do next and right as I finished praying you walked by. I don't care what happens to me. I know what I need to do."

I wasn't sure how to react. This what Laurie had told me about. Amber was willing to recklessly run with me. At the same time, I couldn't just throw her in harm's way. I couldn't let her jeopardize everything. I knew what Laurie told me was true, but I just couldn't put it into practice.

"I-I can't let you-"

"The only way you're stopping me is by physically restraining me, and I know you won't do that."

I stood with my mouth open. I wanted to reply adequately but couldn't find the words. I simply turned and continued walking. She followed.

"Stay with me, and please don't say anything."

We turned onto a gravel drive and immediately jumped into the tree line. We scraped ourselves through the underbrush until the compound came into view. No men stood at the gates, but looking at the buildings I saw men on the roof, surveying the area. At first glance it just seemed like a factory. That's what the world saw.

We continued to make our way toward the back. I pulled out the piece of notebook paper Cameron gave me from my jacket and looked in front of me to see the entrance I needed to make it into based on his poor attempt at directions.

I motioned to Amber that we had to stay where we were until further notice. As soon as my body stopped moving my mind started. I tried to flush all other thoughts and remain focused.

Minutes went by. I entered a state of prayer for what I was to undergo. A peace entered my body and my thoughts became clear.

"God," I whispered, "I don't know how this is going to go down, but I ask that Your will be done."

The noise of tires crunching broke the silence and shouts followed immediately. Two large jeeps burst through the gate and shots echoed in the trees. Windows shattered. The once noiseless place was now a chaotic orchestra of disaster. The men on the roof pushed their positions toward the intruders.

Men filed out of the doors and took cover behind cement barriers and the corners of buildings. Cameron's men came through the tree line, covering both sides.

"Now Amber," I whispered harshly. We burst out of the underbrush and climbed the fence. I turned to help her, trying to balance my care for her and my need to get to the buildings.

We sprinted to the back wall and slipped into the door. Although the majority of the focus was still on the front, I knew silence was vitally important. The building was unfamiliar. Since the group relocated after the previous fall-out, none of Cameron's men had been inside of the new compound. This left Amber and me to guess our way around blindly. We made our way through the bottom level uneventfully. The rooms were either empty or the men were too preoccupied to notice our intrusion.

I led Amber up a staircase to the next level. We walked down the hall that contained windows open to the outside world. The floor was littered with broken glass and the bodies of men who had been shot during the initial attack. I looked out the once intact window panes to see Cameron's men had advanced. However, a group had made their way to the side of the compound and seemed to be shooting at no one. No sooner had I asked myself the question of what the target was when I realized what they were shooting at. The propane tank off to the side of the building exploded, and the second story seemed to lower as the boom resonated across the land. We had walked a ways to get here, but I knew someone had to hear the noise of the blast. The authorities would arrive soon.

The smell of ash began to fill the air as we pressed on. To our left was the last door that remained unsearched. I took the pistol out of my waist band and motioned for Amber to stay back. Her eyes widened with fear. I was surprised she hadn't said anything thus far. I assumed fear and adrenaline had taken a hold of her.

I opened the door and raised the gun without giving it a second thought. A man was shuffling through boxes, stuffing a bag with what he found, slinging the rest to the ground. "Don't move," I commanded.

The man turned around slowly. "Drop the bag."

He followed instructions, maintaining eye contact that expressed all of his hatred.

"Eron, stop!" Amber shouted as she ran up next to me. The man's expression went from angry to confused.

"Amber, now isn't the time. Just trust me."

The man began to look for something, a way to get out of the situation. I cocked the gun and he stopped looking. Amber began to open her mouth to speak but refrained.

I looked into the man's eyes. He was at war with himself. I could see the reality of the situation try to creep in, all the fear and worry. Then the powerful mask he tried so diligently to maintain would return. I knew nothing about his life, but I knew he was exhausted. Amber continued looking at me as well. She never shifted her gaze. I could tell the current version of Eron was not consistent with the Eron she knew and she couldn't reconcile the two images.

Then there was me. My mind was always at war. Yet, my mind was oddly clear at that moment. Whatever happened next was completely out of my hands, and for the first time, I was okay with that.

If I died, I was okay with that. I wasn't suicidal this time. I didn't loathe living. This time was different. I knew what I was fighting for and if I died for that, it was the best life I could've lived. I knew my death would affect people, but I would rather live a short life filled with purpose and living fearlessly for God than a long life of fear. I had found my source spot. It was time I let it affect everything else and let the river run.

"Eron, shoot him!" Cameron yelled as he barged in the room. I didn't pause or look at him as he entered.

"No," I replied as I tossed the gun to the side. The man began to run towards the door. Cameron shouted in frustration and sprinted after the man. Cameron pulled his gun from his belt as the man flew out the door. He left for a moment as Amber and I stood there listening to gunshots.

Cameron rushed back in the room overcome with rage. I began to see the man that Jack's decisions had turned him into. The "New Frank" Laurie spoke of. Cameron. The one that killed my parents. The man that I tried to run from years ago. The man that made me hate myself.

"I knew you couldn't do it. I knew it!" He shouted at me. The flames from the propane had reached the upper levels. The walls and floor began to crumble. "I have fifty men that are risking their lives out there trying to take over this compound and fifty back at our compound relying on us to come back with good news. Do you realize what you've done?"

I paused. I then smiled and held the button on the side of

my G-Shock watch. "You guys get that?"

The voice of the police captain came over the speakers of the watch, "Yeah we got it. Our forces are surrounding Cameron's compound as we speak. Laurie Bentwell has them unarmed and open to extraction correct?"

I held the button as Amber and Cameron's eyes widened. "Yes. Laurie has told them what is going on and they have agreed to the terms, provided they will be unharmed."

The police officer replied, "Sounds good. I'll give the signal. Next door police district has sent a team to come get you. If you can find a way to show your location once they arrive, they'll need that for a safe extraction."

"Got it."

Cameron looked at me with continued rage, yet there was a sadness that had entered it. He was losing everything by the second. The emotions erupted into his voice.

"After I lost my family you were all I had. Did you ever think of that? Did you ever think while you were running around out there trying to be someone else that you had someone that would've done anything for you right with you all along. I tried to give everything to you. I showed you more love than you deserve Eron."

"Cameron, you don't know what love is," I said through a choking breath. "It's misplaced. I thought I knew what love was too. I thought that all I had to do was care about someone a lot and show them attention. But that's not it. To give love you have to have a source of love. Otherwise you'll just be sucking away from the person you're supposedly loving." I looked to Amber.

"Loving someone isn't the selfish idea that someone belongs to you and you can make their life whole. It's the realization that the love Christ shows us is the love we pour into someone. A love that is unconditional, limitless, and is chosen daily; a commitment to choose joy over sadness, peace over chaos, and compassion over bitterness. It's not about the temporary infinities that we think are so important, pleasures or feelings that we want to last for forever. It's about the sacrificial love that makes life worth living in the first place. Because, after all, sacrificial love is the only reason we have a chance at infinity anyway."

Cameron looked at me puzzled. "Well, I don't know about the love you're talking about," he said. He paused as if considering, and for a few seconds, he looked less like the man he was trying to be and more like a man who wanted nothing more than to simply walk away. He dismissed the thought and his expression suddenly hardened. "But whatever I feel makes this a whole lot harder."

Cameron raised his gun at me and cocked it. A split second before his finger pulled the trigger a man leapt from the wall supports and tackled Cameron to the ground. The gun fired as I covered Amber. The two men crashed into the opposite wall. The foundation shook and the rafters lowered as the two men hit the ground and began to wrestle for the weapon on the crumbling floor. The man pinned Cameron down and began to go for his neck until another shot rang. The man on top of Cameron grabbed the gun and threw it to me. As I caught the weapon he released his grip on Cameron and fell to the side. He mustered the strength to get up to a crouch, then to his feet. Blood soaked his white hoodie. He removed the hood, looked at me and nodded his head.

"Thanks for showing me there's some hope in all of this," Jared sputtered out. He hit the wall with all the strength he had sending the rafter above crashing on top of the two men.

"No!" I yelled as I sprinted towards Jared. The air had become ashy, but as I looked at his body below the beam I knew his time was finished. I looked to my left to Cameron. The beam hadn't landed directly but had just pinned his legs. Exhausted, Cameron looked up at the gun in my hand. He laughed sarcastically, coughing through the pain.

"I swear if you find the courage to shoot me after all of this," he began before I cut him off.

"I'm not going to kill you. Amber give me a hand." She ran over and we heaved the beam up off of Cameron. Although she had been opposed to the violence, I could tell she wanted Cameron out of the picture. Nonetheless we each grabbed an arm and began to drag him out of the crumbling room.

We dragged him down the hall, coughing through the smoke. "Amber, stop. We can't drag him all the way out of here. He's losing too much blood. Here." I stopped us by a showering room. "This room is tile and won't burn as fast. I'll open these windows to allow air in. We can set him here until they arrive."

"How will they know where we are?" Amber questioned. I looked down, thinking of an answer.

"Here," she continued, "I'll go out there and lead them

here."

"No way. There are still men out there. I can't-"

"I don't think you have a choice," Amber interrupted, pointing at my leg.

I looked down to see my blood-soaked thigh. In all the adrenaline I hadn't thought about where the first bullet Cameron shot went. I hadn't even stopped to feel anything. As soon as it was pointed out I felt the searing pain and hit the ground. Cameron and I sat side by side in the showering room against the wall. She ripped part of her sleeve and tied it around my leg.

Amber grabbed my hands and placed them around the handle of the pistol. "If you hear anyone walk into this room. You shoot. No hesitations. Okay?"

"Amber you know I can't shoot anyone. It's not in me."

"I don't care what you can or can't do. We didn't fight through all of this for you to die. I know your conscience will fight you. I know this isn't what you want to do, but we'll work through the consequences. Okay? What are you going to do if you hear someone coming?"

"I'm, I'm gonna shoot."

"What are you not going to do?"

"Overthink."

"Right. I'll go get ready for when they get here. Stay safe," she said as she leaned forward and kissed me.

She rushed out, leaving me and Cameron alone. I looked to my left, expecting him to be ready to yell or attack me or something. However, the blood hadn't stopped oozing out of his legs and he had lain down in an effort to stay conscious.

"You want to know why I hurt Jack but didn't kill him?" Cameron asked me.

I looked at him through my peripheral while keeping the gun on the door. "Why?"

"Cause after I beat the man I hated for many years down to the ground. After I surpassed any reason I had not to kill him. After every offer he made me. I realized killing him wouldn't fix anything. I looked in his eyes and saw nothing. Maybe I'm just saying this cause were about to die here, but killing Jack wasn't gonna fix any problems, I'd still be as screwed up as anyone else."

"Hang in there," I said encouragingly.

"Why didn't you kill me? Why did you drag me here when you two could've left?"

I pondered my response. It's when I realized that no response would be adequate that I knew the action I was being led to. I looked down around my neck to the silver chain with the cross from Pastor Reynolds. I rotated my body to a kneeling position, my right leg straight out to the side as the pain seared.

Cameron shifted his gaze to me, unable to move his head. I took off my shirt, tossing it to the side. I then removed the necklace and leaned towards Cameron. I put the chain around his neck and clipped the clasp.

"I want you to have this. I wish I could reveal to you everything I've found, but I know I'm not capable of that. One day, one day you'll understand." Cameron's face softened.

A year ago, I would never have acted in that way. I would have found a way to kill him in the upstairs room. Truth be told, he didn't deserve to live. Truth be told, neither did I. Neither of us deserved salvation, yet I received it. It was only right I extend that offer. No matter what I felt, love overcame that.

My thoughts were interrupted by footsteps. "Eron get ready," Cameron croaked, "there were more men than we could take care of. You're going to have to hold them off."

"How," I yelled "I have a pistol and don't know if I can even shoot."

"Don't hesitate."

The footsteps quickened. I tensed up and aimed the barrel at the open doorway. I had faced a lot of decisions in my life, but this one probably topped them all. It wasn't black and white but puddled with grey.

The sound got bigger and I cocked the gun hopefully for the last time in my life. I told myself that this time was different. I told myself that I was right in this situation. I told myself I had to stay alive. I told myself-

I shot. Amber hit the ground. I threw the gun. Police entered. The noise stopped. I lunged for her. She screamed. I was held back. I thrashed. I was held back. I yelled for her. There was no sound. An officer struck with his baton. Everything went black.

# CHAPTER FOURTEEN

I look up from my notes. The congregation sits before me, eyes wide open. "That moment was twenty years ago," I say. I look to my wife Amber as she sits in the front row, rubbing the scar on her stomach from the bullet that night. "The next few years were filled with regret, trials, and a lot of paperwork. You may have heard all I've been sharing and thought that my life was the worst thing you've heard. But that's the thing. Often times Christianity is plastered as a cake walk, a 'make life easy' ticket. When you look at my life you don't see that. The thing is, that's the life we're called to by following Christ. I hope you all never go through what I have gone through, but the life of Jesus was one filled with rejection, pain, and death. It's not a lukewarm, half-hearted, temporary decision, it's a commitment we carry out daily.

It's the daily bread. And if you have that every day, I think you'll find yourself in a life full of purpose and fulfillment. Because the truth is this world isn't all it tells you it is. If you noticed in the story of my life I skimmed over graduation. I barely even touched my experiences with football. Prom was a blip on the radar. At the time those moments seemed like everything. But when I look back on my life, those weren't the times that changed the course of my life. It was the relationship with Pastor Reynolds. It was the conversation I had with Thomas on the street. It was my time on a boat in the middle of a lake. It was the way God used the world around me.

God has a way of planning your life in a way that you could never expect. Kind of like the author of a book, He knows exactly where you're going while you yourself are subject to the storyline.

I had no idea by sparing Jared's life that he would spare mine. I had no idea when Pastor Reynolds gave me his necklace that I would give it to Cameron. I wouldn't even think that learning the guitar when I was little would come into play later in life. I could never have predicted seeing Amber on that bridge that night or even meeting her.

It's true that it hasn't been pretty, but I wouldn't change a thing. That's a bold statement, but I trust that all of that had to happen to get me to be who I am today. And I'm proud of that Eron.

I know not everything was answered in what I've said. You all may have questions about what I've said or the outcome of events and people that I didn't talk about. That's because until Jesus comes back to reclaim this Earth nothing will have a closed ending. A lot of relationships and battles that were mentioned in my past are still being worked through today. I can think of many people that I wish I could deliver good news on behalf of.

I know my life didn't contain everything. But I can bet that a lot of you here this morning knows what it's like to lose someone. A lot of you know what it's like to be an outcast, to face crossroads, to fall for someone, to struggle to let God take over, to lose friends, to be hated, to lie, to be tempted, to hate yourself. You know what it's like to desire happiness or to want to be proud of yourself. Sin masks itself in creative ways but it's still sin.

If there's anything that I've learned, though, it's that the love of Christ overcomes that. It overcame the loss of my parents, my homelessness, my arrest, my relationship issues, my gang involvement, loss of friends, shooting my wife, and even my suicide attempts. If it can do that, it can overcome whatever you are going through.

I've been fed a lot of lies in my life and it's not easy to know what is true, but let me tell you the truth: there is a God above us that cares more than we can fathom. He loves us more than we can love anyone. However, frankly, we suck. We've messed up. We deserve to die. I deserve to die. Yet, God loves us past our mess-ups, chose to come down as a human, and endure all the same temptations and pain, and take our death so that we can live in Heaven with Him. That's the truth. And it's beautiful.

So right now, I'm going to ask you if you want to experience that. I'm not asking if you want to call yourself a Christian then leave here and go drink your sorrows away, smoke all that you own, indulge yourself in pornography or women, or go drool over money. I'm asking if you want to follow Christ; if you want to leave it all behind for something greater. I'm asking if you want to set your source spot. I challenge you to let the Lord take control of your life.

Please bow your heads with me. If you wish to make this commitment, follow me in prayer.

Dear God, we...I mean, I have fallen short. I have sinned and can't make it in this world alone. The burdens I face are too much for me and I have screwed up and continue to screw up. Lord I ask that You take mercy on me. I acknowledge the way You sent Your Son to die for our sins, and I'm thankful. I ask now as your humble servant that Your Son becomes a part of my life in Spirit. I want to walk again in new life with You. Help me to do that. Help me to be the man You made me to be. Let me proclaim Your majesty with every breath and let each breath You give me glorify You, not turn others away. Please mold me like You, and let me learn what it means to be a child of God. I love You Lord and I give You all of me.

Amen.

Now with every head bowed, if this is a decision you have just made would you raise your hand."

I look up to see a sea of bowed heads. In the midst, a single arm raises slowly into the air in the back.

"Great. You can put your hand down. Everyone may open their eyes." I then feel courage as I have never felt before. God leads my words.

"The pursuit of Christ is one that is reckless. It takes courage. Jesus says that those who deny Him before men, He will deny before His Father. If you made that decision would you please stand up."

I look to the back where the hand was up. The crowd looks around anxiously. Finally, in the back a wheelchair appears in the center aisle. My face lights up. A man wheels his chair down the aisle. His hair is fully greyed and his face is worn. An ankle monitor blinks on his right ankle but he continues shamelessly. He doesn't look to the congregation but keeps his gaze locked on me. He reaches the stage. He then pushes as hard as he can on the armrests and using the arm rests as support begins to stand. He then straightens out his back, shoving the chair forward and with his whole body shaking shouts, "I declared Jesus Christ the Lord of my life."

My face beams. The congregation erupts in applause for Cameron.

"Please see me after," I say. I just told the congregation that the moment Amber asked me to Prom filled me with a joy I wished to have again one day. Today is that day. As much as I would like to simply stand there and bask in the moment, I realize the service must conclude. "Your life is just beginning," I say to Cameron, giving him the same wisdom a dear friend once gave me. Then I turn to the congregation. "Thank you all."

A man steps on stage and ushers me to the side room. After a moment I reenter the worship center and step on stage. The man speaks joyfully.

"Mrs. Basque would you and the kids join your husband on stage?" My kids run up and hug me as my wife joins in on the affection. I motion at Laurie on the second row as she smiles softly before slowly and gingerly making her way up with the family.

"Pastor Reynold's recent passing was a hard moment for us all, but we believe that you are the one he had planned on carrying the torch for him. We are grateful for the role you played in his life and your desire to be a part of this church. With the deacons' approval and a unanimous vote by the congregation we are elated to have you as the new senior pastor of First Baptist Titchadesh. It's what Pastor Reynolds would have wanted and it's what we want. What do you say?"

I look at the congregation. Their smiles beam up. I look down at my family, their love pours into me. I look up at God, praising His name for the life he has given me. I lean forward with all the joy in me, "Yes."

# NOTE FROM THE AUTHOR #2

If you're reading this, you have just finished the story of Eron Basque. Although the story was fictional, the character of Eron and I are very similar. Because the truth is: no matter where you are in life, God will find you. Throughout my life I have met many people. Many of their stories are crazier and more broken than Eron's, yet they all deal will the same idea: a person is born broken and endures suffering, God finds them in the suffering, and they begin to learn who they are and that their life is greater than they could have imagined. However, even though God consistently saves us, we still struggle to say yes. We think our way of life is better and refuse change. We have a preconceived idea of what Christianity looks like and don't want to feel judged. Who could blame you? Many Christians in today's world spend their days in their bubble, refusing to do something about the world around them, or don't live out the faith that they claim to have. Largely it's because Christianity is hard. Sunday school teachers and parents make it seem easy. They make it seem like signing up for Calculus will automatically make you a Math genius incapable of mistakes. But that's not it. Yes, all you have to do to be saved is call upon the Lord to enter your life and accept His gift of salvation, admitting that you yourself are a sinner. We often think of sin as a one-time occurrence, but really sin is a disease that plagues us all. It is a separation from God through our own actions against God. For example, if you are in a relationship and commit an act against the other it not only hurts the other person but breaks the reality of a perfect and loving relationship. We are born into a world full of these acts against God that destine us for death. However, God realizes that perfection is not within our capabilities, so He came down into this world as a human (as a baby named Jesus Christ), to endure the trials that we do, yet continued to live perfectly according to God's commands, and took our punishment by dying on the cross, then rising again in three days to show that He has overcome the world. To put it in another way, it's kind of like if you broke a cookie jar, and you know the punishment for doing so is a timeout. But then when your mom comes out to ask who broke it, your brother says, "It was me. Punish me." He does this out of love and because he cares for you in such a way that he would sacrifice himself in order for you to live happily. Yet, we are still left with a choice. Love is not forceful, it is something chosen. Your brother could not intercede for your punishment if you don't let him do it. God came down as Jesus to take our death, but we have to acknowledge that and choose to love Him and accept the love that He offers us. We have to believe that He indeed took this burden. This is more than a one-time decision. Yes, accepting what Christ did is the beginning, but to truly believe in something is to live your life according to it. If I believe that 2+2=4 then why would I write 5 as the answer? There would be no point. That's where it gets tough: learning to live the life that Christ did, not the one the world tells us to live. The following story is not one that uses metaphors and symbolism. It is bluntly the story of my life thus far. I hope that you find it encouraging to your own life. I hope you find yourself in my footsteps. I hope you are able to let God take control of your own life. You and I are not that different. You may even find some similarities between Eron's crazy life and my humble experiences. I believe this testimony will shed a new light on the previous story and offer a very real perspective on what a life trying to follow Christ may look like.

-Austin Lanning

# MY STORY

Growing up I was a very different kid. I haven't shared this with many people nowadays, but God blessed me with a very high intelligence and creativity. Normal kids spent their days playing little league sports or using their athletic abilities to explore the world around them. That wasn't me. I wanted to explore people's minds. I wanted to write books and stories. I drew the world around me. I wanted to build things.

However, my mind wasn't enough to fulfill me. No matter how many imaginary worlds I created, I was lonely. No one wanted to be my friend. No one understood how I worked. Truth be told, neither did I. Anytime I let my intelligence show I was made fun of. I became angry.

I was angry at the kids around me for not accepting me. My parents tried to raise me in a Christian home, but I had nothing in my heart but apathy for the God I thought I knew. He had cursed me with a personality I couldn't control. I hated Him. My only escape was music. I started taking guitar lessons and writing songs. They were an outlet for the emotions I could never show. I had found a passion.

The anger continued. I began to use violence to solve my problems. I would lash out at my peers for underestimating me. I thought if I picked fights and won I would gain respect. I started using vulgar language to fill myself up. I thought I could use brute force to show the world and God that they were wrong about me. I put on a front to my parents that I was the good Christian kid they wanted me to be but underneath was hatred.

The anger couldn't get the job done. The angrier I became, the unhappier I became. People saw me blow-up and labeled me as a target. They tried to see how far they could push me. Bullying began to become a constant theme in my life. To some people at my school I was in the popular crowd and the people bullying me were my friends. But I was never "in the popular crowd." I was just the punching bag of the popular crowd. They would tell me that if I shoved hot spices up my nose and ate things off of the ground that I could sit with them at lunch. They told me if I shoved my head in a toilet and sent it to them that I could play games with them. "They told me" was a constant phrase in my life.

I saw myself start to slip off the edge and began to scramble for their approval. As I was never picked in a schoolyard pick and my athletic ability was always made fun of, I thought maybe that was the key. I began to scribble down P.E. exercises and workouts from videos and bring them home. My afternoons were spent repeating every exercise until I couldn't continue. I would run my body into the ground, hoping it would become something that people would be able to love. Anything that I could do to get a laugh was within reason. I didn't care what happened to me as long as I had someone I could consider a friend.

Athletics came around. I made the teams. I participated in almost every sport. People began to notice me. I thought I had achieved all I ever wanted. I had made it, but I felt no better. This is when I acknowledged that maybe there was something wrong with me. I decided to turn all the energy I had into hating myself.

That year I was diagnosed with clinical depression. I would put on a front for those at school, smile for the family, then go into my room and cry, tearing myself apart. The thoughts became deeper. The hatred became stronger. I wanted nothing to do with God. My music had turned into suicide notes. I had given up ever pursuing music and decided I was terrible at it. Suicidal thoughts were a daily occurrence. The thoughts became stronger until I tried to take action. Several times I tried to hang myself, run my car off a bridge or into a tree, slit my arms vertically, drown myself, or launch myself into traffic.

I pushed my family away as far as I could. I didn't want them to know what I had become. Finally, one day a guy in my grade invited me to a weekend retreat at his church. I'm not sure how I ended up there, but I attended. I started off knowing no one. The weekend passed and I didn't think anything of it. On the last night we had a service of entirely prayer. Anytime I had prayed it had been a cry of anger or frustration. This wasn't something I was looking forward to. The music began and people began singing and praying. The normal thoughts entered my head saying, "Austin you are worth nothing. Why are you even here?

Your life is a plague to those around you."

But this time there was a new voice that said, "You do have a purpose. If you could let go of all of this anger and hatred, you could see that."

I knew in that moment I had make a choice. I was exhausted. I ended up hitting the ground and saying, "God, I give up. If you think you can do something with my life, go ahead. I give up."

I let Christ enter my life that night. Little did I know; my journey was just beginning. God began this process of rebuilding my life. However, in order for Him to rebuild, He had to tear down. The following two years my life began to change. I had entered high school and I was faced with new friends, challenges, and experiences. In this, I was torn out of my addiction to pornography. I left the screen of lust behind in order to pursue actual relationships the right way. I stopped cursing. I began to use my words to build others up.

This all came at a cost. My first two years of high school also included two ACL tears. My sports career was ending. In order to have my new friends in older grades I lost some that I had grown up with causing a divide. My new relationships with girls continued to fail. I still dealt with the aftermath of my depression and would have moments where I would slip into old habits. I couldn't seem to outrun my past tendencies.

The summer after my Sophomore year I went to England on mission. I encountered many people who rejected Christ and wanted nothing to do with Him. I encountered people who were broken and hurting. I encountered Christians who were struggling to press on in the faith due to a lack of support. That's when I realized that the sacrifices of the past two years were necessary and if I was to pursue Christ, I needed to do so wholeheartedly. The next year was nothing short of beautiful.

I longed for God like water after a hot summer's work. I took up theatre and picked up the guitar again. I realized how special music was and began to play for others. I shared my testimony for others in the church and overseas, sharing the new life I was offered. I thought I had reached a life in Christ. The spring of my Junior year I realized how wrong I was.

Although I was pursuing Christ I had exhausted myself. I was juggling three jobs, school, theatre, church, organizations, and other responsibilities and needed a break desperately. Right in the middle of it was the night a dear friend of mine took his life.

I had spent the night chasing him down, notifying friends and family, and trying to stop the inevitable, and I failed. I couldn't stop it. The community around me fell apart. He impacted so many around him as he truly was a loved friend, brother, and son. Therefore, the removal of such a special person from so many lives was a painful process. Some friends took to the bottle for help. Others wanted to make a similar decision.

A few months later one of the guys that took me in my Freshman year and was a good friend to that day went into cardiac arrest and passed away due to an enlarged heart. He was the perfect example of a man of God and constantly encouraged me to be a better person. I didn't understand why such a blessing to this world could just be taken in the blink of an eye.

I realized, however, that this was what I signed up for. There is joy in following Christ, an indescribable joy. But, like I voiced through Eron's testament, following Christ isn't easy. If my commitment and faith was true I would persevere through the hardships. I would give it all up to God and trust that in the end I would be alright.

Due to my commitment to Christ, I wanted to spend my days exploring God's world, investing in others, or trying to better the world around me. The majority of my friends wished to find their joy in other things. Many found that the bottle was a way to bring them happiness for a little while. That is, until the bottle was empty. Then they would wait for the next opportunity to try again. Others found drugs to be their sense of peace. They found that it made the world bearable. Girls, sports, video games, and work took the rest away. Because I didn't participate in the same activities, I found myself alone. I don't say this with judgement, but with sorrow. I know what it's like to lose yourself to the world. I know what it's like for the world to take pieces of you with it. I found myself right back with the way I was years ago. But I'd never let them know.

I'd never tell my friends how lonely I felt. I'd never tell them how I cried the nights I found out they lost their body to their boyfriend or girlfriend. I'd never tell them the nights I'd stay up praying that they'd see the big picture. I'd never tell them how their words tore me down still. I'd never tell them that although they thought I was friends with everyone now, I really had no one. I'd never tell them that I was unhappy.

I had to keep loving them. I had to keep trying. It wasn't until the spring of my Senior year that it finally hit me. I wasn't back where I was years ago. I had lost people because I was taking a different road than most. I had felt out of place in the world because Christ calls us to not be of this world. Life was hard because that's what I was called to. This was the life I chose. I couldn't blame anyone for the way I felt. They made their choice and were on their own path. I would, however, keep loving them. Because the truth was, I didn't deserve salvation, but I received it. Now it was my job to extend that to them. Judgment is not my place. Frustration is invalid. Anger is misplaced. Hatred is pointless. Yes, I need to let emotions out. I should never keep it all bottled up. But I should never hold onto negativity as I do not know or understand enough to make that kind of call.

People need each other, whether we know it or not. The very people that would push me away were the ones I was called to love. I am not living on my own desires but according to a greater plan.

Looking back at my eighteen and a half years of life, I feel at peace. They haven't been perfect. They still aren't. I still screw up and will forever be a work in progress. Whether people were by my side or not I am thankful for them as they made me who I am today. I apologize to those I have wronged or pushed away. Loving without limits is difficult and I'm still learning how to do it. I apologize to those that I have hurt or neglected, that was never my intention. I hope that if I have wronged anyone that they can find it in their heart to forgive me.

Most of all, I hope that those I have encountered find Christ. I hope that we can mend our differences and that they can rejoice with me in the lives that we live. I hope that at the end of our days we can stand in Heaven and look back at our lives, not as perfect but as headed in the right direction, constantly striving for something greater than ourselves.

Whether you are Eron Basque, Austin Lanning, or somewhere in-between, I hope that you always know that there is a God above offering unconditional love greater than what we can comprehend. All you have to do is say yes.

# JOURNALS OF THE DAMNED

Lanning

# NOTE FROM THE AUTHOR #3

The following are un-edited journals that I have written throughout my high school years. I labeled them the Journals of the Damned not because my life is painful or awful, but because we are born damned to die, as sinners. Christ offers us another route. The following journals express my confrontation with that fact and my struggles in following the life of Christ in a world so broken. I placed them in order. You should be able to see my growth as a person and a series of highs-lows. Many of them are low points. Once again, this is not because my life is awful but because, like many of the Psalms, they are an expression of pain, joy, confusion, or frustration. All of these are personal to me as they are written about me directly either in a literal sense or as a metaphor. I hope that you appreciate them and identify with them and know that through all of them, God has been good and is always going to be good. Often the darkest ones were when I did not understand. As I am writing this, the show "Fixer Upper" is just ending. In it houses are remodeled. The stars of the show are so good that when the audience sees the house before they do not look sadly at a failed house, but get excited at how the stars could possibly turn a broken and damaged building into something beautiful. I challenge you to read these like that. Truly this is what Christ does with us. He takes our brokenness and makes it better than ever before. Don't let a day of sadness outweigh the joy of your life. You are still beautiful yet.

With love in Him,
Austin Lanning

# Dear Future Me
December 24, 2015

Dear Future Me,

Every day I think about how my future will turn out. I dream of traveling the world, releasing my own music, publishing my book, finding true love, changing people's lives, being happy. I want to say that you'll have done all of that by the time you read that, but I know as hard as I try, my future isn't in my own hands.

I hope that you've started to live how you want to. I hope you've given up on trying to please your parents and elders and that you're pursuing music and writing because I know that's what truly makes you happy and at peace. Adults have probably continued to tell you to go to Medical School, or Engineering School, lecturing of how successful you could be. But I know your heart lies in your imagination, so quit trying to complete someone else's reality.

I hope that you've realized you can't make everyone happy. You can continue spending all of your time and money trying to bring other people joy, but you can't please everyone. So I hope you're still not disappointed every time someone turns their back on you or leaves you out in the rain, but thankful that you had the opportunity to meet them.

I hope that you've found true love. I hope that God has placed someone in your life to show you what you couldn't see before. I hope she's the woman you've always dream of, and that you're treating her like a queen every day. Never take her for granted, if you start to, remember the time you wrote this when you'd give anything for someone to show they love you at all. Fight for her. Never let her go.

Finally, I hope you're happy. You know I don't mean that lightly. I hope you've finally learned to love yourself. I hope your heart isn't heavy with self-hatred. I hope you realize who God made you to be, and no longer yearn for a release of this life. I hope that you're laughing every day, and not faking it. I hope that you're smiling, and not forcing it. I hope that your relationship with Christ is without any doubts. I hope that you are finally confident in who you are, and no longer want to change yourself daily. I hope you're happy with the life you live, and living a life that makes you happy. I hope that you have hope at all.

Sincerely,
16-year-old you

# Insignificance
## December 25, 2015

Christmas is a turmoil of jumbled emotions. Everyone looks forward to the day, but when it comes around, it never meets expectations. As the years go by, our excitement becomes smaller. We watch our childhood and emotions slip right out of our hands like a greased rope.

The gift of our Savior is so great. I can't help but feel worthless. Jesus laid down his life for me and yet I acknowledge the idea like a friend saying hello. The actions of our Savior should be with me like my own skin, going everywhere with me, displayed for the rest of the world to see. However, I feel that I am ungrateful still, and that I'm missing something. I feel that I'm truly understanding like I wish to believe. Even the physical gifts I feel I take for granted. My parents who have already given so much. My Savior who has given His life. Yet I remain here barely able to give a card.

I'm not doing enough. My actions thus far are insignificant. Yet I lack direction. There are so many cracks to mend, but no instruction on how.

So I smile, thanking everyone for the gifts and for the company, yet my heart feels empty.

So I give, hoping they will like the gifts, when I know they deserve a gift so much better than anything I can do.

So I cry out, knowing I have accepted Christ and surrendered, yet lack the feeling of the unconditional love He offers.

So I fall, emotionally exhausted into a deep slumber until next Christmas arrives.

# False Identity
December 27, 2015

Friendship is a word that is easy to define, yet hard to experience. Many relationships that we believe to be strong, are built on broken foundations, with deceitful ties, and topped with empty promises.

Almost everyone seems to be living for themselves, driven with selfish desire. When around people that need to be used, the mask is put into place, making everything seem genuine and mutually beneficial. But as soon as the back is turned, the true intentions and emotions are brought out into the light. Yet the friendship continues until one is satisfied or the misplaced trust is broken, and the cycle repeats.

Not everyone is like this however. In a sea of deceit lies islands of love, compassion, and the art of being selfless. They offer safety, closure, assistance, and most importantly love. The clothes off the back of these is given if necessary, and the roof is shared when needed. These people are there when needed and when not needed, providing an endless blanket of compassion. Yet these people lack the "important traits" of society. They are used as doormats for those who need to climb higher as they lay helpless, continuing to offer love to those who cast them aside. So the waves of the sea crash against the islands, tearing away their land, altering them forever.

So I sail through life. Gazing at the beautiful waters, being lured into the depths before I realize it's too late to turn back. I observe the rugged islands, knowing they will offer security that need, but lack my attention still. So I sail on, wondering if the risk of being hurt is worth the coolness of the water.

So I sail on, wondering if going against the majority of the world is worth the benefits of security and love.

So I sail on, endlessly frustrated, and wondering if I really have control over the boat at all.

# You
## January 4, 2016

I want you to be the one. I want you to be the one that can make me happy. I want you to be the one that can show me what it means to be loved. I want you to be the one that changes everything.

All my life I have been a worn-down path. People use me when they need me, but no one ever takes the time to tell me I'm appreciated, no one ever tries to repair me, and no one ever cares that I'm there. But I know you can be different.

Truthfully, I don't know if I'm falling for you, or the idea of you. But truthfully, I don't know if there is truly a difference. I want to give all I have to you, yet I don't want to push too hard and lose you. I want to be with you, yet I live in a constant fear of never being good enough.

Your beauty shines like a gem, beautiful yet strong. Your smile radiates to others like the sun bringing them warmth. Yet I am a mess, who could never be worthy of such a masterpiece. Your kind heart shows love and happiness to everyone around you. Yet I can't even love myself and would not even know the mere meaning of happiness.

There are so many problems. The doubt rips me apart. But there are so many things I desire. My heart yearns for a strong Christian relationship that I know is tangible, yet unlikely for someone like me.

As much as I want from you, there are things you want from me. That is where I fall short. I give all I have, yet it is never enough. I fear pain, as I fret it will be the last straw to my unstable mind. I want to be the best man I can for you, even though I don't know myself. I want to be everything you need and more. I want to make you happy. I want you to feel loved and appreciated. I want you to never doubt yourself. I want you to realize how amazing you are. I want you to feel like I never could.

So my mind fights itself. Torn between desire for you, and doubt for myself. Wanting to be with you, but afraid that you could never feel the same, and that the balance will tip, until it finally falls over, breaking on the floor.

I am afraid. I am nervous. I am yearning. I am fighting. I am paranoid, that I will over think the situation further, ruining what could have been.

I am stupid. I am a mess. I am no good. I am asleep, with dreams of you keeping me sane, until I realize that that is my reality and my desire for peace with you draws me into further frustration, until I break down in indescribable emotion.

# Torn Pursuit
January 26, 2016

What started as a joke, became serious
What started as nothing, became something
What started as a want, became a passion

I never am one to admit my feelings. Whether it is my dogmatic mind or the inability to face the truth, I remain resistant. Yet I can't deny the passion within me to be with you. And the passion to make you happy.

Every moment someone is showing you affection, is a moment I wish I had seized. Every time someone is with you, is a time I wish I could have took part in. Every thought that goes through my mind, is one that is filled with you.

Yet I hold back. Knowing that you will be gone soon. Trying to accept that you will most likely never feel the same. Yet I don't want to accept that. I want to continue on.

I want to be with you. I want to make you smile and make you laugh as often as I can. I want to hear all that has happened to you in a day's time and how you want to spend your days to come. I want to make you feel happy and loved and that all will always be okay.

I want you.

I want to take you places you've never been. I want to give you all I have to offer. I want to make you feel like you never have before. I want to explore the world with you.

I want you.

I want to grow in faith with you. I want to become a better person because of you. I want to serve God with you.

I want you.

You.

I want you, and everything that comes with it. Your nervous laugh when you don't know what else to do or don't understand. Your eyes that crinkle when you smile. The smile that makes me return in doing the same. The smile that makes my day brighter. Your eagerness for all things. To learn, to live, to love. Your heart that bursts through when you talk or laugh, displaying passion with every word spoken. Your faith and how it shows with how you live your life. Your morals, your independence, and your views on everything. I want to listen to your problems and hold you when you cry. I want to look up at the stars and talk about the future that we think we have planned. I want to shine with pride, and yet humility when I look at you, thinking, "this amazing woman is mine."

I want you.

Yet I feel dumb for wanting you, never believing that it could happen. I feel dumb for thinking you could care for someone like me, be with someone like me, love someone like me. I remain too afraid to confront my feelings, scared I will lose you forever.

So I lay here torn between a disbelieving fear of what could happen and a passionate desire of what I want to happen.

Until you leave.
Then the time has passed.
And I remain distressed and broken over words unsaid.

I want you.

# Time
January 31, 2016

Time is the most brutal captor created, and we're all imprisoned. It molds our society, listing who we can be and who we are forbidden to become.

I want a loving strong relationship to sustain me, yet time tells that such a thing does not exist at this age and I have to wait to meet my true love at a later time.

I want to follow my dreams, yet time tells me that I must complete an education first and will not be taken seriously until a later time.

I want to experience the world, yet time tells me I am too young to go off on my own and that I will not have the money to pursue that ambition until a later time.

I want to voice my opinions, changing the world and its' views. Yet time tells me I am too young to have an opinion and cannot voice my ideas until a later time.

I want to leave this place. Yet I am told it is not my time.
I want to find the love of my life and begin my future, yet I am told not now.

Not now.

Why put off something that is reliant on an indefinite source?
Why waste time constantly if it will soon run out?
When will I find these answers?

Not now.

So I remain in a constant struggle against society, destiny, and myself, with time holding the ropes restraining me.

Until I slip.

And I look up to realize that it was me holding the ropes of restraint for the entirety.
But it is too late.
Time has run out.

# Shangri-la
February 24, 2016

In a life full of suffering, I find myself dreaming of a perfect life----a place that stays in my imagination, no matter how hard I try to make it my reality.

I dream of a life where I'm not expected to follow a path--A life where I'm not laughed at for trying to create a path of my own. A place where I can truly do what I love, and love who I wish, without letting everyone down.

I dream of a life where I look to my side at friends that became family, rather than worry if they're here to stay for the week. Where I'm not walked upon but am able to walk hand in hand with them, knowing that I will never be alone. Knowing that these people won't leave my life like the rest and will show me a love I've never known.

I dream of a life where you love me. A life where our love sustains us. Our kids look up at us and from the beginning know that one day they want a relationship like ours. You look at me and don't see a broken man, but one born again. I look at you in marvel at how I ended up with such a beautiful woman that I could call mine. I don't know much but I know I want to give you all you've ever wanted, show you the world, and sing you to sleep every night.

I dream of a life where I'm good enough--where I'm no longer the runt of the litter. A place where I don't feel like failure, afraid of success because I know it won't last. A world where my voice and ability is enough, and I'm given the chance to make my music and write my life out before the world to hear. A world where I'm not held back.

I dream of a life where I can love myself. A place where I can release my doubts. Where I'm not dreading every day. Where I'm not wishing it would all end.

I dream of a life without all the sadness.
I dream of a life where I've found love.
I dream of a life where I've found happiness.
Where I look forward to the next day, believing the possibilities are endless, excited as to what the world could bring before me next.
I dream that it could stop being a dream, and that I could find peace other than in my sleep.
I dream that I won't have to wake up.
Because eventually reality tears down us all.

# The Infinity Cycle
March 2, 2016

It's tough fighting a losing battle. Giving all that you have, yet deep down knowing you can't win. Yet, you keep trying unsure why you waste your energy and time on it. In that moment you realize, it's all you know how to do.

It's more than just a battle. It's a cycle, one that seems to go on forever. An endless loop of disappointment and despair that shows no release. You fight, and you crawl along, just to be stomped on again. It never ends.

Yet it's strange. Sometimes it seems that the one person that can release you from that cycle is yourself. You don't allow yourself to feel love. You don't allow yourself happiness. You don't think you deserve it. The slightest glimpse of hope is shattered by your own hand. Why? Who knows.

You continue fighting this battle against yourself, unsure of what side to take because each part is a part of you. How can you ever truly win against yourself? How can you get a release from your own grip? The question remains.

You are me.

I pour my sweat into an occupation that serves no benefit, in hopes that maybe it will be enough to pursue my desire to preach to a world that doesn't want what I have to say.

I pour my body into a mold that I remain unsure that I even want. Starting from the beginning over and over. Learning how to walk, how to run, how to exist, over and over, with progress never apparent.

I pour my heart into a woman that will never be able to fathom how much I care. Being in love with someone that will never feel the same simply does nothing but tear you apart further. But I continue to love because it is all I know how to do.

I pour everything I have left into staying alive. Fighting my inner demons, fighting the part of me that I wish was not. I push against the wall, not to break through, but just to stop it from falling on top of me, consuming me for all eternity. It is all I have the strength to do.

Why can't I find safety? I've prayed and plead more than anyone will ever know, yet I'm still here. I give all I have fighting this losing battle until I collapse out of pure exhaustion. So I'll continue on, finding safety and happiness in the rare moments I can, treasuring them as long as I can, because it's just a matter of time before the cycle begins again.

# My Prayer
March 3, 2016

Dear God,

I don't know where to begin. I feel that my prayers get repetitive, missing the point of it all. So God please help me to focus on You. There's so much to this world good and bad, it makes it hard to focus on what's truly important, as temptation consumes us all.

I feel that I never thank You enough. Whenever I come to You I am always asking. Yet I was given a family, a freedom to worship You, good health, and I was given life by You, yet I take it all for granted. Thank You for all that You've blessed me with and I'm sorry for not always recognizing that.

God, please help me find my purpose. It seems as if I walk aimlessly through life. Pursuing everything available in hopes that it may be the one thing I love to do and what I was made to do. Help me recognize that and pursue it. All my life I've been told that my talents need to be used practically, and never for the imagination, yet the world of dreams is where I belong. Yet, I know not of how I could ever support a family, or glorify You through that, so please God, help me find my calling in this world.

God, I need to admit, I want to want You, but some days it seems so hard. I know I should desire You, and rely on You, yet daily I try to fend for myself, only seeking counsel when it all crashes down. Please help me to come to You first for all things, because I know You are the only one capable of truly controlling my life. Help me to have a new desire to follow You every day, displaying Your love for everyone to see.

My future seems so clouded, and it's tearing me apart, God please give me patience and assurance that all will turn out according to Your will. Daily, my stress builds up until it is too much. Daily, I worry about where I will attend school, if I will pick the right major, if I will get the right job. Daily, I worry about whether I'll find true love, whether I will find the one, whether I will have a successful family. Daily, I worry about whether my kids will love me, whether I will raise them right or not. Daily, I worry that I'm not being the Christian man I need to. Please God take me and guide me, the more I worry the more I hurt, and I need You to take that away, I can't handle this life alone.

And God, please, please, please, help me for those times I feel alone. Help me let myself feel love and happiness. Guide me to the fountain of happiness and love so I can drink finally after thirsting for so long. My mind and body grow weary from my inner battles, and I need You to heal them. I want to feel secure, and loved, and wanted, and needed, and safe in Your presence Lord, please show me what to do.

I don't know what to do, and I need You now more than ever.

I thank You for the many chances You've given me, and the opportunities to try again. I've fallen short so many times and continue to keep falling short, yet You're still here. God thank You for not leaving me, I know You know all so You can see how much I need you. Please ease my pain, and keep me fighting, and keep me glorifying You. There's so much I've still left unsaid, but I know You can see my heart and I know You can understand my troubles more than I can. So please God, hold me and let me know that all is well. Because I no longer know what to do.

Please God, I lift all this up to you,
Thank You,
In Jesus name,
Amen.

# Everything I Didn't Say
March 26, 2016

There's so many things I want you to know. So many feelings I wish I could express, thoughts that I can never convey.

I want to let it all just tumble from my lips, everything that is inside of me that is driven towards loving you. Yet I can't.

You remain longing for something you once had and it tears me apart. The way he hurt you, the way he neglected you, the way he ruined the meaning of love for you. I know I am not worth much, but I could promise that I would love you with all that I have.

I wish that I had gotten there before any of the others. I wish I was the man that changed everything. Seeing you cry because of him hurts me more than you will ever know. Yet I must remain a friendly encouragement or else I will lose you altogether.

I've tried to move on, I've tried to respect that you will never feel the same, yet I take one look at you and fall in love with you all over again. No matter what you've done or what you will do, my feelings remain constant, and all I want is to give all I have to you.

I wish that I was good enough. I look at the guys you pursue and chase and I instantly strive to mold myself into that guy for you. If it was something you sought, I would go anywhere to find it. Your beauty leaves me breathless every instance like I'm seeing you for the first time. I don't know what we would talk about or where we would go but I know that I want to spend every second with you.

Everything around me is telling me no, yet my hurt ignores the signs and yearns on. No matter the consequence, who I am, or who you are, the only thing that appears clear to me is you.

Yet I hurt, every day, knowing that I will never be anything to you

# Seeking
March 29, 2016

My heart beats fast. Every word spoken strikes me as if the sound waves are going through my body, shaking my heart. I begin to shift nervously, my body twitching. I try to wrap my hands together and feel nothing. I look around at everyone, wondering what they're thinking, wondering how alone I truly am, wondering if they can sense my thoughts.

The silence slowly absorbs the room, blackness overwhelms the vicinity. I begin to do all I know how to do. To run. My feet quickly move towards the door, my head never thinking to turn back. I walk down the hallway, knowing exactly where I am going, yet I have no idea why. I hit the always locked doors to find them ajar. The building is desolate and I am reassured that something is happening, that something will change.

I enter my destination. The room is dark. The pews are empty. The stage is vacant. The only lights are a few that dimly shine above the ceiling high above. The cross on the wall is slightly illuminated. I stop.

My heart slows down. My body is overwhelmed in tranquility. I step slowly towards the alter. No sound is present, no disturbance is near. My mind fails to race, as it stays in its place, vacant from thought for the first time.

I reach the alter. And I cry out for God to speak to me, I am lost, I am hurting, and I won't let anyone help me or love me, I do not know what else to do. I am silent.

I wait patiently for a response. A sign, a feeling, anything to lead me. I wait for clarity, for help, for strength, for anything to guide me. I am silent.

Time goes on, and I begin to struggle. Thoughts of life enter my mind. Distractions and irrelevant ideas storm through, leading me away from my state of solitude. I try to fight them off but the feeling is gone. I am frustrated.

I cry out my struggles. The pain I feel daily loving someone that doesn't care, and the stupidity I feel looking for happiness in a relationship. The frustration I feel giving all I have to friends that cast me away like trash. The discouragement I feel giving everything I have to make others happy because I cannot find happiness myself. The confusion I feel when looking for God and never finding, and then blaming myself for not being good enough. The distress I feel when I refuse to love myself or accept that anyone else could love me either. The hurt I feel when there is nothing left to fight for. I am broken.

I wonder what the point of the occurrence was. I wonder why I am here with still no prevail. But I continue to seek, because nothing of this world can change a thing, so I know there must be more. I am human.

# Overthinking Imaginary Thoughts
April 23, 2016

What if this is all for nothing. I've fallen so many times, with a new scar to show it. I've fallen so many times, and each time a piece of me is left behind. Each love takes a shard of my fragile heart with them, leaving an emptier chasm inside than before.

What if this will be different. I fall to find there is someone to catch me. My fear is extinguished, diminishing the flame of doubt. She returns the shards, making me whole again, to a happiness I have never known.

What if the truth is deadly. I fall to simply find the arms I thought were there were in my head. No one is there. No one cares about me like I thought they would. I am alone once more. All of my love and passion has been set out to simply get walked over and ignored. I send the letter containing my heart, waiting for a response, when it had been cast away like garbage without a second thought.

What if this tips me over the edge. As the ground beneath me is ro moved, she is the last stone upon which I stand, once gone there is nothing keeping me from falling into the abyss. Everything has been taken away from me. Everything except for her.

I cannot live in ignorance forever. What if I am too late and miss my opportunity? What if I rush and force things that are not meant to be? What if I overthink it all until my own thoughts consume me?

What if I could simply leave it all behind?

# Timing
## April 25, 2016

My feet dragged along the worn-out tile as I carried food back and forth. My legs ached from the day and my eyes drooped from the lack of sleep I was experiencing. As I passed by a booth in the corner, an elderly lady asked me to grab her a napkin. I thought nothing of it and followed my directions. As I walked back the thoughts of the past week bogged down my mind. All of my failures, all of the pain, all of the sadness. It overwhelmed my every action.

I returned to her and she began to speak, "you know what I noticed? How everyone here is eating with someone yet doesn't care about what they are doing or who they are with." The waiter facade fell from my face as her words caught me off guard. "Everyone is so caught up in their normal lives that they never take the time to appreciate the smaller things." I nodded my head in agreement. I agreed completely with what she was saying as it has always been my belief to stick to simplicity, yet I shuffled nervously as I knew I had tasks to complete and would be yelled at soon. I needed the promotion they talked to me about. I needed something good to happen.

She spoke again "Even you, I can tell you want to have this conversation badly, you need someone to talk to, yet you're still worried that you'll disappoint those around you and you're busy in your own thoughts about everything going on and whether you'll be yelled at for talking to me." I stopped and looked at her quizzically. All my life I've had to constantly explain my actions and why I do what I do just to have no one understand me. Yet this woman was seeing through everything I was.

"Sometimes at restaurants I sit alone and just look at everyone to try to find the person that isn't affected by this selfish world we live in, I look for someone that's different. And now I'm talking to you. You see I'm 77 years old, I probably have 5 to 6 more years left, yet, I'm okay with that. This world continues to disappoint me. I went back to college 4 times with four different occupations as an effort to keep up, yet after a while I realized, it's not the new things that are turning this world, it's the people using them. Yet, if people can change the world for the worse, there's always someone that could turn it for the better. I can see you're hurting so let me tell you something. I had a student from the Bahamas a few years back that had a scholarship for track. But he injured himself and lost everything. They cut him off without even a doctor's appointment and sent him back to his home country. The next year he competed in a world meet and got second. I kept in touch with him and he was picked up by a North Carolina coach from the Caribbean who understood him and gave a full-ride scholarship. He's now making $600,000 a year with a family in wealth management. North Carolina is the only college that offers a degree in that--" At that moment my manager tapped me on the shoulder requesting me to get back to work. As I walked off I looked back at the woman. "I'm sorry our talk got caught short, but the point was, bad things are going to happen that aren't understood. But sometimes those things are necessary to create opportunities for better things to take place."

I smiled and thanked the woman walking back to my area. Thinking about what she said. Realizing that you can't understand something sometimes not because the problem is greater than you, but because the problem is a part of a grander plan than anything you can ever think of.

# Derailed
May 2, 2016

I told myself I wouldn't fall again
I told myself I would stay on track and not let emotions guide my way.
I told myself it was nothing.

Yet here I am. With you in my arms, wishing this moment would last forever. Looking up at the sky talking about life as if we have any grasp on any of it at all. Every time you speak, I absorb every word, the sound of your voice slowly melting my heart. You look over at me, the moon light glinting off of your eyes and I know I could not find a more beautiful woman if I searched for all of my days. We lay under the stars, the wind whistling around the train underneath us, as your head rests on my chest, and everything I could have ever wanted was with me.

Yet all paradises are mirages.

Life resumes. You get caught up in what's to come and what goes on around you, while I think about us and what could be. You become worried with the stress of life, while I imagine a world where you have fallen for me, and your eyes look admirably up at me, and I am all that you need. You begin to focus once again on the priorities of education and social connections while I am distracted by the image of your beauty. You are concerned with your past, and look back at it all regrettably, while all I want is to take that pain from you and replace those memories with ones of happiness and love.

Yet I told myself I wouldn't fall

I tried to hold my guard. Yet with every breath you broke it down, pulling me closer. I did not want to feel again, yet I now find myself wanting to write all the words in the world and sing them to you. I want to show you the world and the beauty of nature that you've never seen. I want to make all things possible for you. I want to make you happier than you ever thought you could be.

Yet even though it was me holding my guard, I am the one whom fears the future.

I don't want to lose you, yet I am not enough for you and want you to find someone that is. You deserve the best, and I am not that person. You deserve someone spectacular, and I am not that person. You deserve someone who can be all that you need, and I am not that person. Yet I try every day, to be the best man I can for you. Even though my efforts may all be in vain.

Everyone questions my actions.

No one will support my emotional ambitions, so I cling to the hope that this isn't all in my head. I cling to the hope that maybe there is a possibility. I cling to the hope that you could ever care for a man like me. I cling to hope because it is all I have as I fall for you, unsure whether there will be someone to catch me at the end.

# Peace
May 5, 2016

Sometimes in the middle of a storm at sea, it's hard to see you're almost to shore.
Sometimes when you fall face down, it's hard to see the bullet fly over your head.
Sometimes when you can't seem to make the pieces fit, it's hard to see they belong somewhere else.
Sometimes when your problems get so big, it's hard to see the stars above and realize how small you are.

The past remains the past because it is what you have passed by. It was there for a moment, and then gone with the rest. It can be remembered, or reflected on, but it is not meant to be lived in.

We are all a part of something greater than ourselves, therefore we should not be surprised when we can't understand it. We crumble under stress because we are not meant to hold it alone.

Mistakes create cuts. Cuts create scars. Scars fade. They always remain, but the pain is gone. They simply stand as a reminder to what once was, and what should not be again. The sting is gone, the ache has been left behind with the memory. Your body has continued.

If everyone accepted your ideas and who you were, everyone would be the same. There would be no "friends" or "opportunities" because everyone would simply be as each other. It takes bad to recognize good, as it takes hate to realize love. One cannot exist without the other.

Sometimes it takes the darkest nights to notice all of the lights brighter; as light can only shine through a broken vessel.

You do not need to feel others' love to be loved. As you do not need to be others' happiness to be happy. A life fulfilled is one driven by passion and kindness. No day is promised, no time is guaranteed. You can't change the past, and you can't control the future, therefore all focus should be on the present.

In a world full of practicality and logic, dreams can be lost, ideas can be forgotten. However, when one man has the courage to not give up is when history is made. Thousands of men follow each accordingly and receive no recognition, but the one who creates his own path is the one that changes it all. Some dreams are meant to be yours because no one else may understand them.

But they exist as a seed. Nothing can force the plant to grow, nothing can alter what is, but eventually rain falls, eventually the sun shines again, and the plant continues on to its fate, regardless of any attempts.

Live with love and love the way you live. Some may cross a puddle for you while you remain stranded in the sea trying to get to them. But a day spent loving another is never a day wasted. It's not self-neglect, or a void, it's fulfillment from loving others as you were shown by a God greater than yourself.

Humility creates awareness. Awareness creates a purpose. Purpose creates a passion. Passion creates love. Love creates a life. And that life brings peace.

# Walls
May 10, 2016

I'm sorry.

I have tried to hold on. I have tried to just be. But a tortured soul ceases to rest. What I desire I know not. What I need, remains a mystery. But I have tried and failed.

Whether it is those around me, or the one whom I cry out to, or the medicine coursing through my veins. I cannot reach happiness, and I cannot fathom satisfaction.

I have tried letting down my guard. Laying down my weapons in hope for a loving embrace over a painful battle, just to be taken advantage of until I am barely alive.

My actions please no one. My words remain lost desires. And my being remains a failure. The storm has been on the horizon, its path inevitable. I am ready. For what I do not know, but anything can be better than the present.

I have tried.

Through nights of tears and overwhelming fears. Through infinities of pain, and through moments of going insane I have tried.

I patch the holes. But the water is stronger than I. Living in a world where your dreams are shattered like my confidence. Trying to be good enough for a world that sets the bar right out of your grasp. Casting out your love to have it trampled upon.

I have tried to stand against the current but it has taken its toll. I am weary, and those that once offered support have kicked me to the ground and moved on to their own successes.

I'm sorry but I have given up. Let the waters take me, whether I land in the purest of fountains or off of the falls I know not, but I have accepted fate as it is.

# A Path of Progress
June 19, 2016

When things remain dark and hopeless you begin to become comfortable. You remain unsure of whether you really want anything to change, yet in the pit of complacency God finds a way to pull you out of the depths. As I pursued happiness continually I had little hope that it would be found in England. A country without God and love seemed like it would be a heavier burden on my weighed down heart.

I was wrong and I thank God I was.

As I leave the great town of Bramhall I cast my eyes over the English countryside and am finally satisfied. I feel fulfilled and full of purpose, a feeling that was once unfamiliar to me.

Entering the experience worries filled my mind and troubles strangled my hope, yet I consistently prayed for peace and patience. And whether I believed I would see results or not, instantly God took the reigns of my life. All my worries were taken by God, my spirits soared to new heights, and I felt needed, and helpful, and it was incredible. No concerns of mine mattered in a life that was not my own. I simply got to watch God's work for myself.

My doubtful mind usually searches for faults or failures yet I look back and the only word that comes to mind is perfect. God's love is perfect. He took something broken and didn't just fix it but used it to fix others.

Going back, the normal life will continue, and the stress and craziness of life will resume, yet it's okay. I have a God that can bring peace and love like no other. And I feel that whatever is thrown at me will be embraced and used for positivity. I may not know what the future will bring, but I finally have the peace to accept that and let God control what happens. Life is too short to fill with stress and sorrow. I thought control was what I needed, but it was the thing I needed to let go of the most.

# The Wanderer
June 29, 2016

I stand on the soil packed hard beneath my feet, in the middle of unfamiliar lands. I look behind me, I see mistakes I've made, things I could have done better, failures. I look ahead and cannot see my hand held out before me as the fog clouds all that lies in wait. I think about where I came from, and continue to move forward, as it is all I know to do.

I make it through the trials, I survive the wilderness around me, just to move on to a different unknown. However, no matter what I face, or how much suffering lies ahead, I would rather send myself away then face settling. Where there is settlement there is reality. Where there is reality, there is my true self. I am proud to say I no longer fear myself yet it has been replaced by a fear of fear itself, which has kept me at distance from all that I once knew.

I remain moving through people like I am under surveillance, afraid that if I stay too long they will become worried at what lies underneath. I indulge myself in new places because the familiarity of my own home has brought negative feelings I do not understand, and like all people I run from what I do not know. I have failed at happiness, love, satisfaction, and all that is necessary, so I run, in hopes that the chaos of the world can disguise my own chaos within. I pursue acts of adrenaline and adventure and fearlessness because the day that I begin to fear, is what I fear the most.

My thoughts lie in a complex design that even I do not comprehend. I cannot explain so many things and don't understand myself to any degree, yet a balance is found. Everything is held at an equilibrium, yet the scale tips.

Closer........ Closer.......... Closer, until one day the scale will spill, and the cracks will widen into chasms. Yet I will run and wander, and when it all comes crashing down, I will be too far gone to be affected by the impact.

# Beautiful
July 8, 2016

Eventually all chaos comes to a close. Eventually all waves die down. The world is brought back to an equilibrium and the calm covers the earth like a warm blanket of peace.

My eyes scan the landscape, savoring every moment because we know not when we will receive another one. As the sun reflects off of the river below, and the shadows touch the trees, all is well. Yet as the stillness initiates my thoughts, my mind wanders to the possibilities of the world that lies untouched. And in that moment, I know I want to experience it all with you.

Everything that is beautiful in this world reminds me of all that you are. It is not a description of physical attributes, or social charm. But a presence of beauty that overwhelms all that stand in the way. It sticks out over all in comparison due to the world that wishes it could claim right to the creation of you. Your beauty is one handcrafted from God intended to be a masterpiece among people. I lose focus at the sight and fail to come up with words that come close to describing all that you are and all that you represent. I could write all that could possibly be written and have the words simply bounce off of the surface because your beauty is one that reaches depths intangible. I pray every day that you are able to see the graceful work of art I see and think of yourself as the life changing woman I think about every day.

I hope that I will be enough. I hope that you might find charm in my words or see the passion behind my trembling face. All I aim to do is be all that you need. You deserve a love that is unfathomable. You deserve a love that is unwavering. You deserve a love that is bold. You deserve a love that is beautiful.

# Chaos
September 26, 2016

There used to be comfort in the chaos
Life seemed as if living in the eye of a hurricane was possible

But eventually your body must stop, and you must reflect on who you've become. To realize that you have embodied the chaos in yourself.

Time goes on as my hands reach backwards desperately trying to undo the ropes I have tied. Yet, as I strain and strain, I do not know which ropes to undo, and which ones I should have never messed with in the first place.

I have lost touch with who I used to be. And I don't know if I'm happy with who I've become. I have continued on, I have made it here, but at what cost is my fear. Many have been left behind, many have been hurt, and many stay idle waiting for what I will do next.

The chaos I have ensued has overwhelmed me. When I am without it, I desire it once more. Leaving a mind that tears itself apart in multiple layers of thought and passion.

As I write I struggle for the first time to find words. Twenty-six symbols may be able to identify the world around us, but even an infinite number of symbols cannot capture the essence of my troubled heart.

I'm sorry. I never meant for this to happen. I'm sorry. I let my own happiness and success create chasms between us. I'm sorry. I am different than those around me and am diluted by my own dreams. I'm sorry. If I have hurt you or made you question yourself. I'm sorry. For who I have become.

So I lay. The chill of the earth beneath me clouds the emotional ache with physical discomfort. I fail to make a plan as my mind fails at every task it receives. I loathe the idea of thinking about anything as I loathe my mind itself. I cannot focus, as I am torn. I cannot mend myself, for this is how I was born.

So I lay, for whatever chaos comes next.

# The Full Circle
September 30, 2016

My legs churn furiously over the worn-out tile as my mind darts from one thought to the next. Constant worry and stress surges through me with every move. As I carry the platter food in front of the counter I see a face; a familiar face. I ignored the possibility and continued on with my duties.

I returned in the same path, darting to grab the next order, when I noticed her again. I had made no mistake. I paused at the sight of a woman I had not seen in years. Her slender face and distinguished features connected a faint memory to a present encounter. In confusion I slowly spoke her name.

Her eyes lit up. A smile spread across her face as she shouted my name with glee. I stood there quizzically. This woman and I had once had one of the worst relationships a teacher and student could have. Growing up I filled my classes with ignorant remarks, disruptive behavior, and constant defiance, leading to a child hood of punishment and failed relationships with teachers. My mind went back to all the memories we shared. She believed in teaching symbolism and deep thinking, which I understood, but still rebelled against as I did not see it's usefulness. I treated her with more disrespect than almost anyone, so to hear her jubilantly call my name with glee I was astounded. Yet I smiled back and hugged the woman I had once pushed away.

"I thought I saw you as an escort during the homecoming pep rally! I called your name but I was too quiet! It's amazing to see how much you have grown!"

At this moment I had to settle my restless thoughts. "But, I thought you hated me, we didn't exactly have a good relationship all the years I spent with you. I figured you couldn't have cared less if you saw me again."

Her jaw dropped and she began to speak in a passionate tone. By each word she sounded more like a proud mother. "Austin, you've got it all wrong. I do remember all the times you disrupted the class, or how I would walk down the hallway to always see you sitting outside another door due to your misbehavior. But while the other teachers became frustrated and dismayed, I knew. I knew why you were the way you were. I may have yelled or gotten frustrated but I never gave up. I saw the way ideas and thoughts clicked in your head like a network of webs only you understood. I had just hoped that you wouldn't give in to the peer pressure of those around you. I hoped that you would never abandon your uniqueness. Speaking of that, what are you doing nowadays? Are you going to be an engineer or doctor or something?"

I stood there astonished at her words. I began to understand. I looked back and it all rang true, this woman was the only one that embraced me for who I was while the other teachers casted me to the side like a pest problem. "I'm a Junior now," I said. "And no, I'm actually looking into something with writing, music, or maybe even ministry."

Her smile widened. "I'm so proud of you. That sculpture you made me in the eighth grade that you said symbolized life and its relation to the battle of purity vs chaos? It's been sitting on my piano ever since. It reminds me of you. It reminds me of possibility."

At this moment her daughter's name was spoken by the cashier and she stood up to go grab the food. "I'm so glad I got to see you, keep me updated on your life, because I have a feeling you're going places even you don't realize."

I smiled. I had been thinking about her and those classes for the longest time with regret of who I was back then, and wondering if I was any better now. Yet God decided it was time for my past to be resolved.

As she walked out the door waving and smiling, I said goodbye and told her I would. Yet, I meant it. I wanted to tell her about my life, because even though at one time she was the reason I hated it, I realized in that moment that she was the reason I continued to live my life how I did at all.

# Abandoned
October 11, 2016

The cuffs clip around his arms. He doesn't resist, but simply allows his body to be slammed on the front of the cop car. His eyes wander up to the abandoned mansion in front of him. His shoulders slack. "Too far, too far," he mutters under his breath. The policeman stands him up straight and stares into his eyes. "I don't get it," the policeman stated, "what are you trying to find in places like these." The youth pauses then meets the officer's eyes. "Myself."

The tension in the officer's body releases as his eyes ease into confusion. The winter breeze rolls through creating an atmosphere of utter silence. "What do you mean son? Have you been using illegal substances tonight?"

The youth grins for a mere moment before dropping back into a state of direness. "I wish it were so. The answers would be much easier to find. But if it were so easy we wouldn't be here tonight. These buildings hold history. At one time they were cherished and important. Some were even restored for a period of time. But in the end nature takes over, and the foundation loosens. The frame rots. And we are left with an empty shell of what once was.

When a building is discovered once again, it is given another chance to bring someone else happiness and interest. It is given a purpose once more.

And in this moment of discovery we realize we are walking in a world much older and larger than ourselves. As we are outlived by a compilation of sediments. Yet the forbidden always appeals to those it is restricted from. The adrenaline courses through the body, reminding us we are alive. Reminding us that there is still life to be found. Reminding us that an empty shell can still be filled. Reminding us that there is hope.

In the dullness of our lives we yearn for fulfillment. We yearn for someone to give us a second chance." The youth stopped and stood there just as before. The officer stared at the young man puzzled yet amazed. This surprise soon turned to doubt. "That was real nice kid, but I'm not buying it."

The youth shook his head at the officer, "You won't buy it because you've always lived buying something else, and you're afraid to change. You've come too far to lay down your pride for someone you feel superior to. You're led by a feeling of self-confidence, believing that you know best. You lead yourself to think it is your duty to be here. You believe that undoubtedly all of your decisions are justified through a cemented guideline believing in no gray area, just as I believe that my decisions are justified as well. Yet you still believe that you are simply doing a duty given by a superior, never giving a second thought to the idea that maybe your encounters with those that oppose you have more than one purpose." The youth stopped once again as the officer began to anger. He stepped forward towards the young man.

"As an officer your goal is to eliminate all evil. But you can't succeed in that by detaining everyone that opposes your view. Life isn't about shutting those who differ out or bringing along those that believe the same. It is recognizing our differences as people and using them to strengthen, not tear down."

The officer began to get frustrated. "I've had enough of your rambling, no spiel is going to disguise the fact the way you're living your life is wrong."
The youth held his ground and spoke one last time, "that's fair, but who are you to determine which way of life is right?"

The policeman launched at the young man. With a yell he slammed into the ground. He picked himself up off of the ground in confusion. His feet stood on the old wooden panels as his hands ran along the abandoned mansions walls. There were no police lights, no youth, no arrest. Just him. He turned around to see a bathroom mirror. Pinned to the mirror was a picture of him and his pregnant wife. He turned around quickly astonished and angry. His wife. His future son. Next to the picture was a handwritten letter. He leaned close to the glass, reading the scribbled lines,

"Dad, I know we differ, but don't let your personal perspective disguise the possibility of another way. Another mind. Another hope. We all struggle with our own battles, but whatever happens in them, don't abandon your fights. Don't abandon your goals. Don't abandon yourself."

Love,
Your Son

# Dear Present Me
November 23, 2016

I'm sorry, my heart goes out to you truly. But I say these words out of love, nothing less. It is not words of comfort but what needs to be said. After all, I do know you the best, you are me.

Pick yourself up. You've been treated unfairly I see. You've been hurt I can tell. But you know, no matter what happens you will keep on loving. Crossing oceans for those that wouldn't cross a stream for you. But don't be discouraged by that. Your actions mean more to those around you than you know. Do not base your worth on the feedback you receive, but on the fulfillment, you feel knowing you've done right.

After all it is in your head you see. The thoughts you believe they possess are nonexistent. The only one who contains those thoughts about you is yourself. Take the negativity you keep wrapped around your heart and use it for good, think of the positivity you could bring.

Even if you are correct in your assumptions of how others feel or who you are, it matters not. Eloquent words are not needed here. Pick yourself up. Walk on. It will never get any better loathing in misery. If you truly want change that has to come from you. Do something about it. Make up your mind that you are going to finish what you started and the destination is worth the journey. Keep fighting.

For every flaw there is a multitude of blessings. Find joy in the breath you take. Find power in knowing you are not alone. Find peace in being assured of who you are and that you are enough.

No more sadness, no more pain, no more suffering. Just pure determination, happiness, and love.

Quit writing this and read what you have written. Take your own advice. Leave now and make the most of the time you have left as it is forever fleeting. Goodbye friend, we will talk again soon.

# Soldier of Life
January 19, 2017

The cups were a blur as they tossed about in my tired hands, the weight of the day slowly pressing down with the force of exhaustion. My mind had grown numb to the present and forgotten what it was like to be calm and fluid as every movement was replaced with a vial of stress.

"So are you still in high school?" I heard a man say behind me. My eyelids closed forcefully as I knew I was about to produce meaningless words to a man that would forget them the next minute. Yet as I flipped around I softened. A young African American man stood at the register leaning against the countertop. Although he had ordered out, he showed no sign of hurry or any burden for that matter. His eyes seemed to bounce as he smiled at me, simply happy to be alive.

"Uh yeah, I am. What about you?" The man looked to be about 18 or 19, yet with the youthful glow he had about him anything older would have been an oddity. "No," he chuckled, "I've been out for four years now."
Naturally I returned his response, "So what college are you at?"

"I'm actually in the Marine Core," he said. Yet he said it as if it was a normal college. The smile on his face wasn't fazed and he sat there as if he was an ordinary guy. "So I'm guessing your awaiting deployment if you're in Waco," I suggested.

"No I actually just got back from being deployed for two years in the Middle East. We were sent up to Russia to infiltrate but ended up in Afghanistan where we were engaged in firefights with ISIS, although I was stranded on one of our boats for a while after they attacked."

I stopped what I was doing and looked at him with a new wonder. He spoke as if he was telling the story of how he went walking with his dog, yet every sentence was more courageous than the last. Yet the smile remained and he looked at me lovingly like a good friend.

"So you're back now? What's next for you in all of this? Cause honestly I feel kind of dumb just wasting my time serving sandwiches," I spoke in a joking tone. Yet, there was more truth behind it than he knew.

He laughed. "Don't feel like that man. I'm over there because that's my battlefield. That's where I need to be. Your battlefield might be right in your home country. That doesn't make it insignificant, just different. It doesn't matter whether you're a soldier, a lawyer, or a waiter, if you're living your life with purpose and making your impact on this world then you're already winning your battle. As for me I committed to 20 years of service." My eyes widened. He continued, "there's nothing here for me, that's where I belong. Serving and protecting the ones that can find something and use it for the greater good, that's what I do."

People came into the doors towards me as he grabbed his bag. His eyes met mine, yet it was no longer a look of envy, pride, pity, frustration, or even the joy I had seen at the beginning, a bond of respect was linked between our eyes. I thanked him for his service. With that he nodded, turned and walked into the night, as I was left to find my battle, and to find something worth protecting. Whatever that is and wherever it may be.

# Going for Broke
April 17, 2017

"Keep going," my foot slams the gas pedal to the floor.

"There's more, there has to be," I tell myself as the road turns into nothingness, uncharted territory.

"You've gone too far to turn back, seize this moment while it's yours," I continue to entice myself. As my mind goes for broke, the meaning takes full swing and the pieces shatter.

The adrenaline has left my body like water that has been dried in an instant. And my body forgets what the affects of the toxicant were. Although sense and reality crawls in, my body still yearns for more. I am left on the pavement with no regrets, and no consequence. My mind understands what has happened, yet doesn't know how to prevent another, as it is already looking for a new escape as this reality will never sustain it.

"You can make that." My feet cling to the edge of what I know where I began. In front of me lies what could be, the goal. In between is a chasm of inevitable doom and defeat. Yet the feeling rises up again. My feet itch for a new place to stand as the old area has been fulfilled. My knees bend and I launch towards the hope of a better tomorrow. My body slams into the side, I only hold on by the tips of my fingers and pull myself up with all that is within me. It is done.

The thoughts of the possibility of the past do not exist. Only the content satisfaction of a risk worth taking lies within as I move past the previous decision, and my eyes scan for the next challenge.

"This can't be all there is." The same words that created the greeting now say goodbye as I move towards somewhere. The same words that initiated a love of power now powerfully dismantled the word. The same words that carried me to where I needed to be decided that destination much be changed. My gut holds on to my mind and with tight reigns and I become unsure whether this is my faith in God talking or the impulse to acquire what is better than what I have. Or is this the youthful ambition I must keep to succeed in a greater way than anyone else, a usually dismissed thought process that could be valuable yet. Immaturity, some call it. Maybe they are right.

As the realization hits I run out of destinations to reach, I have no love to fill the void, I have no more hellos to give or relationships to make, I am alone. All have been driven away. Every opportunity is now sunk with the ship while I lay stranded on this island of frustration. Yet hope keeps purring along with my heartbeat, there is more still, I can start over. The cycle continues. Until finally the gears overrun and the engine overheats. My body fails to function. My mind has been exploited. All that is left is a carcass of the past spirit. The carcass falls. Going for broke had achieved its goal. My body has been broken. And finally, obliterated, until no one can fix it, and the spirit of unrest has finally found what it was looking for all along.

# Thoughts
April 27, 2017

My eyes stare into themselves in the clear glass, where all is exposed. The edges of my mouth quiver and my body begins to shake. The muscle I had spent years to build means nothing and I fail to even stand.

My past has become my present. I've already experienced this, I've learned my lesson from this, why is it coming back. What more do I need this for. I don't want this.

I tried to mask the cracks. My ship had finally made it to open water and was sailing. Yet, now it seems that a storm has started to brew. I can feel the waves beneath the hull, it is familiar. I know it will only get worse from here. I try to prepare, but can I? Or is it pointless to try to avoid the inevitable. But I don't want to stand here idly, waiting for the crash, but I must.

These thoughts have returned, options that were never apparent before have become reasonable, and that terrifies me. Who have I become, and how can I stop myself from becoming something different?

Even as I write this I know none of what I've written will make sense, it is simply conflicts of my mind. As I sit in this dark corner with the rest of the world but a foot away, I wonder if there is hope yet. But for now, I cannot handle the alternative, so I'll sleep as it is my only haven.

# The Story of a Girl
May 12, 2017

I don't want to mess with relationship, I don't want to mess with things that shouldn't be tampered with. Yet every one of our expectations as people is met by a countering force, one that promises to flip what we believe to know.

But I find, the less I worry, or force, and the more I allow God to execute His plan without my interference, the greater the outcome.

Then there's you. As I expect my day to be another time period following a set standard, you break my routine. As you walk up to my business to address a friend, the expectations I once had are now gone, and I am truly living; taking each moment as it is. Your smile instantly electrifies the area, shining brighter than the reflection on your glasses. The exchange of words is short and brisk as you head back to your routine, yet I know our cycles have now acknowledged the presence of other ones, and I will see you again.

Time grants me another opportunity, which I am certain to seize. The certainty of isolation has dismissed any possibility of this growing, yet here you are. There is no chance of you falling for the person I can barely call a man, yet here you are.

I want to go further. I want to see what this has in store. I want control, yet there you go.

Life goes on without you. I go on with it. This time I am not the one left behind. The year comes to close, and you appear once more. I gaze into your blue eyes as your smile lights up every emotion inside me. I'm left at square one.

The stars align and the music plays, but I can't. I fear once I fall there will be no returning from where I have come from. "If it is meant to happen it will," I tell myself. I let you leave. I let you walk away. I've given up so much of myself so many times for nothing, I can't do it again. Not this time.

Time progresses again. The new year creates a new beginning for me. I find another. I fill my life with senseless business to create artificial emotions. I put myself through pain and challenges, which soon turn into despair.

The death of a loved one breaks the plateau plunging me deeper, and you appear at the rim of the pit looking down. I wonder if this is what it takes to see that you care. Part of me needs you to move forwards, the rest of me shuts you out.

It is different this time. You do not walk away. We grow. Things change. I change. I believe in the possibility of exceptions and the possibility of hope. Maybe it's time I let someone in again.

Time goes on and so do we. We have become a consistency for each other.

Time goes on. You stop it. You cut the stem before it could blossom. The flower falls into the dirt, ready to be taken in by the earth it came from. You try to fix it, but every attempt shoves it deeper into the soil until it is impossible to get up again.

I wonder if I should've fallen earlier; if I could've tried harder, if I had let you in earlier, if I had taken advantage of the time when I had the chance, if I had been better. The attempt that took it out of me has pulled all that is left.

Time goes on, so do you, but I stay, laying on the gravel circle made of rock as broken as I, surrounded by the life and growth of grass. I wish the earth would take me like the dead flower, as I know I cannot grow again. But time goes on, leaving me to question and regret all I ever did. I question the day I met you and every day after. The blue eyes that led me into another world. The blue eyes that lifted me up, just to let me fall down to the earth below.

# Empty
May 21, 2017

Is this what I was destined for? To be a pitcher.

I am filled with love. I am filled with joy. I am filled with strength. But I am nothing if I contain it. So I pour myself out to any container that comes near me. Every last drop until I am empty.

Empty chairs.

I wait for someone to want them. The moment someone chooses them they are fulfilled, but no one can sit forever and soon they are back longing for someone once again. They fear that no one will; and that the restaurant will close, and they will forever be neglected.

Empty wells.

They were once plentiful. They served so many and gave life to anyone nearby. They were necessary. But time outlasted them and they are now left to waste as they can no longer be what they once were.

Empty ruins.

The failed attempt at adaptation. They tried to serve a purpose that was inevitably deemed a failure so they tried to change accordingly. However, the pattern repeated. Yet as the building constantly changed to serve new demands, the foundation weakened. Each expenditure damaged part of the structure, until it finally crumbled as it was not worth the space it took up.

I am all. Yet as I lay, an empty shell of person, there is still you. I look at the flesh that is all I have. I can spare it. I don't need this. All that remains is yours.

As I sign away the last of me, the hand of which I sign begins to disappear. I realize my predicament. In order for those around me to live, I must cease to exist. In order for them to thrive I must weaken.

So I slide down the slope grabbing for a handhold that isn't there, and I brace myself, for the movement from empty to nothing. The movement I was destined for.

# Auxiliam
June 3, 2017

I am unsatisfied with the life I have, even though I have no reason to be. I lose myself in feelings that fly away at the whisk of a hand. Who I am seems to be contained in a taxi, rushed off to wherever it's needed, containing something different each time. I search for adventure in every moment because I'm not happy with who I am or what I have and hope to God there is more. My mind races like an uncontrollable hurricane, tearing down its surroundings in the belief that it will be all that it needs to be in the end.

In the end,
"Austin why don't you decide what you truly want then let me know," she said.

"One day you're going to realize all you needed was right here. Everything's going to fall apart and all that's gonna remain is us. I can't wait for that day," they said.

"Why do you travel around the land searching for something all the time, what are you trying to find?" He asked.

"You're the strangest person I've ever met. I don't know how someone lives the life you have. There's no one quite like you," they all said.

"I've tried to find you, but all I found was more questions. I don't know who you are, but yet I don't think you know that answer either. I can't put it into words. If you tried to paint a chameleon, that's what it's like to try to love you."

My adventure has brought me back to my starting place. I don't see another path, so I keep tearing through underbrush, driving miles upon miles, and walking on rusty ladders.

"But Austin those ladders might give out. You might get arrested. You could not make it out."

I hope I don't.

I've built this house. I've put myself into it. I believed God was the architect of the plans I was carrying out. I did the most extravagant things to piece it together. It looked beautiful. My house was beautiful. Now I've realized it was built in the wrong place.

Do they only love me for the temporary fulfilling adventures I've found that I can share, or do they love me for the me I can't figure out? Is it possible to love me when I don't know who "me" is? I have so many dreams and so many aspirations, but I can't handle the reality of today. I have so many words I want to write and so many emotions to express, but each breath is a struggle.

My journals have even lost their layout and depth. They have become cries of anguish, failed attempts at love, and jumbled thoughts of my sorry excuse of a mind. This is all I have anymore.

Words on paper.
The prayers of my fading breath.
The passion I have for her.
The memories and experiences of the adventures of the past.
All I have.
I hope it will be enough to make it another day.
It has to be.

# Outside In
June 11, 2017

I sit back exhausted in my chair, staring into the interrogation room. Through the panel I see everything: every move, every breath, every thought, yet they don't even know I'm there from the inside. I've seen so many people come and go, it's lost its charm. All that remains is a cycle.
"Austin the woman is here. I think you'll recognize her, you've dealt with her before," I'm informed.

Instantly a name pops into my head, it could be no other.

You walk into the room and my head hits the glass. I can't do this. Not again, not now. The first officer steps into the room. Intimidation and violence as his weapons, he lashes out at you. You scream and cry out. But I can do nothing. It's my duty to sit on the outside, it's my curse to watch what's within.

With every cry I match pitch. With every tear three of my own fall. As my hair grows tired from being pulled out he leaves the room.

"Please let me go in there," I ask. "I know I can do what needs to be done just trust me. Give me a chance." "No," I'm told. "Not since the last time." I'm forced to sit and watch you in there alone.

The man renters. He begins resuming his previous tactics, yet now your emotions are being abused. I see the tears happening within your body and the memories that will turn into nightmares. I throw my chair to the side and begin banging on the wall with everything I have. Tears run down my cheeks as neither you nor him seems to notice.

"They can't hear you. Your battle is pointless."
"Let me in there!" I scream. "I know what to do. I know how to fix this. She doesn't deserve this, I can do it please," I beg.

"We have a different approach," I'm informed.

The first man leaves and a second takes his place. This new one is more physical. Yet instead of intimidation, he is pulling different strings. I'm repulsed by his actions yet right as I begin to relax I notice your attitude change. You begin to ease into his way of thinking. His actions are no longer resisted. I don't want to watch this. This isn't who you are. I know it's not. The relationship between the two changes as I look away.

My head is forced back to watch. "STOP." I yell. "This isn't her. Get him out of there!"

"A little longer."

My body collapses in frustration as I endure the entirety. "Please let this be over. This isn't the solution. She needs someone different. She needs someone who cares for her, not power or her body. She needs me."

"She does need someone like that. And we've already found one."

My jaw drops. This is worse than the violence. This is worse than the seduction. A charming man enters the room. He simply sits down and begins a conversation. You smile. I hadn't seen that in forever. You laugh. Something I've failed to make you do. As it continues my spirit dies inside. I had lost my opportunity to enter that room. I deserved this. Yet it was torture that I never knew existed it. My exhaustion is overwhelming as I have been punished relentlessly. The two in the room stand up, and walk out together, hand in hand. I bang on the glass one last time. It doesn't move. I look around the doorless room in defeat, and crumple. As another life as thrived and succeeded, mine has left me once more.

# Torn Pursuit Pt. 2
June 25, 2017

It's been over a year and everything has changed, except this.

Caring for you has become like breathing. I don't even think about it. It's second nature. With every moment comes a blink of an eye, a raise of my chest, a flicker of movement, and a thought of you-- and a stab to the heart.

Every time I think of you it is followed by a rush of disappointment as you're something I can't have. Yet, even just to be a part would be enough. Even just a piece. Yet, I can't get any closer as I know I'll get burned.

I try to brush past, fill my mind with thoughts of other.
I satisfy with a replacement, you shatter it.
I lose myself, you find me.
I cast myself to the other side of the world, you follow.

As the options run out, so does time. I count down the days until we are separated, yet I don't want that. I want to be by your side. I want to be enough for you. I want to shelter you with love. But I can't. And you won't.

It's been over 365 days.
Over 365 days of you finding a way back into my life.
Over 365 days of you becoming more beautiful every day.
Over 365 days of you making the wrong choices and I have to watch you make them knowing I could be the right one.
Over 365 days of pain as I can't see you without falling apart inside.
Over 365 days of trying to get away, to move past this...in failure.

Maybe it's just who I am. Maybe I'm in love. Maybe I'm an idiot for thinking I even know what love is.

So I'll keep counting down these days. Not in hope that you'll leave. Not in hope that you'd ever care for me. Not in hope that you'd see the beautiful woman I do. Not in hope that I'd be enough for you. But in hope that I'll wake up and breathe, without a thought of you, without pain, without knowing that my day will be one in over 365 of an endless cycle of chasing after you.

# לְהַנְתִהְל
## August 2, 2017

God said, "My son, take this bag. Carry it to the cliff side from which you were reborn by me."

He placed the bag on my shoulders and it immediately sent me crashing to the ground. "God you know the path better than I. I can barely make the journey without such a burden, with it would be suicide. What's inside?"

He replied, "Don't worry about the how or why, just rest in the fact that I am God and will deliver you from these trials."

Begrudgingly I stood. Step by step I left the mountain top using all the strength I could muster. As I neared the edge of the summit I gazed out in the distance and viewed the cliff barely visible on the horizon. "There's no way." I told myself. "God this is too big for me. It's too big for you."

As soon as the words had left my mouth the ground underneath gave way. The bag and I plummeted down the mountain side. Rocks flung into my side, digging into my flesh. The sides of the face slammed my body, brushing every inch as if condensing the volume of my body itself. Until finally I was left at the bottom. Unable to breathe. Unable to move. Unable to function.

God said, "this is what would happen if I were not with you. I am giving you what you need to accomplish this."

I screamed. "God if you're the kind of God that sends someone through a series of excruciating pain to prove a point I don't want to serve you."

"You have it all wrong my child. Due to your choices you have arrived here. If you had not chosen to stand there and question me the rock would not have broken. I am protecting you from the troubles of this world, but when you question me and choose your own path you stray from mine, sending you into difficulty."

"Fine," I replied. "I'll do it your way."

I continued on. There were moments I cried out to God when I was feeling away. There were moments where He walked beside me, and I felt His presence stronger than ever. Days went by. Followed by weeks. I had become accustomed to the way things were. Then slowly I felt Him less. In return I prayed less. I depended on Him less. I became used to the silence. But I kept trudging through the landscape as I knew it was my goal and I had come too far to turn around. Until eventually I came to split in the path.

In the middle stood a sign. One pointed to the cliffs. The other pointed to my hometown. It pointed to safety. It pointed to all I felt comfortable with. It pointed to security. In the near distance I could see the rooftops. I remembered memories of my happiest moments from within. And to the cliffs just a steep incline up another mountain. My body ached. I hadn't slept. I hadn't ate. I had relied on God for necessities but since I hadn't heard from him the normal instincts had returned. I began to walk towards my home.

"No." God bellowed
"What do you mean no?!" I yelled
"That's not the path I've given you," He replied.
"I don't care anymore! The path you've given me has been nothing but pain! I want to see my family. I want to see my friends. I want to see the people that make it worth it!"
"No," He answered. "Trust me."

"Trust you?! For weeks I've lugged this heavy sack around and you won't even tell me what's in it! That's it I'm seeing what's inside." I threw the bag off my shoulder and began to untie the rope around the opening. But before my hands could loosen one knot I was struck to the ground.

I was sitting in a chair facing a screen. The screen came on revealing a younger version of myself. Dangling from the cliffs I had been heading to, the younger me was barely gripping a small branch. He screamed curse words to the sky as he blamed everybody for his predicament. To his left was a rope ladder. I shouted at my past self to just look to it. To just grab it. But his anger and emotions blinded him. With each shout the branch cracked more and more until finally he relaxed. "Alright God! I give it up to you. I'm the only one to blame for why I'm here. My life is yours."

God replied, "Austin I didn't put you here. Your desires did that. I'm not forcing you to do anything. Look to your left. This ladder has been here the whole time. If you could've let go of what you thought you knew you'd have seen it." My past self-climbed the ladder to find no one there and walked off. I pressed my face into my hands at my own stupidity.

I woke up lying next to the sack where I had left it. I picked up the bag, turned towards the cliffs path and continued on. It was time I started learning to trust. I continually prayed to God, not just when I heard back from Him. I learned that true faith was trusting someone regardless of how things were going. Finally, after more days of tribulation I burst into the clearing by the cliff and dropped the bag.

Screams entered my ears as I ran to the edge. I looked down and saw my family. I saw my friends. I saw those that made it worth it. "This is why I couldn't go home," I told myself. "Unpack the bag," God told me.

I ran back to the sack and quickly undid the ties and the bag fell open. Out came a rope ladder. On each rung a different name was written. Some I didn't know but as I got to the base they began to become familiar until finally it got to people that had pulled me out of my depression and darkest moments. "God what is this?"

"It's all of those that have come before you. That suffered before you. And that have trusted me, thus resulting in saving you. Now go."

I ran to the edge and threw over the ladder. The nearest person was close, but not quite close enough to reach it. "God it doesn't reach!"

"Have faith. It's missing a rung reach into your pocket." My hand flew into my pants pocket and pulled out a rung with my name on it. I tied it to the end and lowered it down as my family began to climb up. "But God, there's so many. Not all of them are on ledges some are hanging like I was. I can't get to them all. I can't save them all!"

"You don't save anyone. That's my job," He replied. "That task is given to no man. Love and trust is a choice, not mandatory. I am using you not to pull them up yourself, but to give them hope in that they might pull themselves up."

I looked down to see each person begin to reach into their pockets. Slowly, one by one they removed ladder rungs and attached them to the sides. One by one they pulled themselves up over the edge. I looked down at the sides of the ladder and scribbled in blood on the rope was the name "Jesus." I smiled as I thought about how I almost gave up so many times. I laughed at my own doubt.

As I turned around to pick up the bag and head home it was gone. I looked around until I spotted the purple bag on the shoulders of my friend as he headed off towards the mountain top.

# Real Emotions, Artificial Reality
October 10, 2017

"Hey man, so... are y'all a thing?" My friend asked. Motioning to the girl asleep in the backseat.
"No," I replied, not making eye contact.
"I know that look, what's going on. You want to be, don't you?" He questioned. I looked down glumly.
"Man, I feel like she looks at me differently. I mean you all say I'm a Christian guy with the highest morals, which in some ways is great. However, it's like it scares people off. I'm not a saint, I'm as messed up as the next guy. And man, I know the odds are against us, time seems to be hard, and her past seems to be weighing her down but ugh, I don't know how to do this. I don't know how to be the guy she deserves, but I know three things

1. She's the most beautiful woman I've ever met. Every time I see her my heart jumps and I fail to come up with even one word that captures that feeling. It's the feeling when you've just won the big game. It's the feeling when your favorite band comes on stage. It's the feeling of adrenaline coursing through your veins... but better. She is mystery to me that I can't wait to solve, and I kind of hope I never do. Her heart is one of the deepest I've ever encountered, and it gives beauty a depth greater than seeing the ocean for the first time in person. Every moment spent I'm already feeling the excitement of receiving the thing I spent it on. I don't know how to capture her other than just saying she's spectacular.

2. Her scars don't make her broken, they make her human. I don't know where this will go. Obviously, I want it to be meaningful and to last but I don't know what God has planned. I'm just thankful for the moments I have been given. But let's say it does work out. Something beautiful blossoms and it turns into love. That's a commitment to overcome anything, even past mistakes. I know she's hurting. But I want to show her what a Christian man is like. I pray that I can be that. I want her to see what

she truly deserves, not what she's had. I want to bring her closer to God. I want her to see the beauty in life and in herself. I want her to know that she is enough as she is and that I can't promise perfection but I promise effort in that I'll try to be enough myself. She has skeletons in her closet and so do I. Let's work through them together yanno?

3. Relationships have been explained to me as hard but pursuing her has been the easiest decision I've ever made. I don't know what tomorrow will bring, but this is what my heart is telling me so I'm gonna follow that. I may land flat on my face and I probably will, but hopefully at the very least I'll have impacted her and she'll know there's someone that truly cares for her. More than any guy and deeper than she knows.

I don't know man it's a tough situation. But just to know her has been a blessing, and I'm excited to see where it goes and the spectacular woman she's continuing to become."

I looked in the rear-view mirror to see her smile. She didn't say anything but I knew she knew. A smile spread across my face.

I look up from the paper I had been writing on, the smile being the only real aspect of the story. I look down at the words I had poured out. My smile slumps down to a still expression. I sigh, crumpling up the paper of a car conversation that never happened. Full of words I could never say. I toss the wad in the trash and walk away from the desk, leaving my emotions there.

# The Empty Chair
November 5, 2017

I sit back in the chair that's supported me for so long. My shoulders slump down as if my arms are being pulled towards the ground. My chest rises and falls slowly with each shallow breath. My eyes stare blankly at the empty chair in front of me.

Many have sat in it, but all have left. For years it was desolate and the hope that one day someone would take it had gone. Right as I was about to leave though, someone finally took the seat. I was no longer alone. The place had been filled and the table's purpose was complete. I began to gain confidence in myself and in my own purpose. Then one day, the person left. The chair was empty again. Time went by.

One day another person claimed the chair and sat in it. My emotions raised up again, adrenaline courses through my body. I was complete again...until they left.

The ride continued as the chair was occupied then left once again. With each change the chair was worn more and more. Wear started to breakdown the table and all surrounding it. With each new person that sat down, the emotions changed and the feelings lessened their intensity. After a while, I didn't want people to take it anymore, as I knew they would leave soon.

Finally, I blocked off the chair. I didn't want anyone to sit in it. People would walk by and I would look at them, expecting them to keep walking and to find another. I would not get hurt again. If the chair were to get taken again, it would have to be worth it.

One day someone walked by. Someone special. I began to look, to dismiss, until I stopped. Something was different. I found myself undoing the blockade. I had opened up the chair one last time. I looked expectantly, in hopes that it would be claimed. I wasn't sure if what I was doing was right, but it was too late. The seat was taken. However, the chair had been through too many visitors as soon as the person began to sit down the chair broke. The wood splintered and fell to the ground. The person ran away leaving only a pile of rubble.

So now I sit. Staring at a pile of once was. A history of pain and wear. No one would sit here ever again. I had risked the last seat to the wrong person. I look at the pile, sadness weighing on me like my heart is being pulled down into my soul. The feeling of listening to a sad song intertwined with history was a glaze over every thought that entered my mind. I stare blankly at the past, living in the hope of what I didn't do. Breathing the breaths I once had. My heart raises up into my throat as I wish to scream a cry I can't afford to give, at once it leaves, it won't come back either, and my voice itself will leave. So I stare in silence, hurting, and swelling, hoping for nothing as nothing remains to hope for. Nothing but remains. Remains of an empty chair.

# House of Cards
December 28, 2017

A torn pursuit is something I'm all too familiar with. It's the epitome of every person that's been introduced to my life. Desire plagues my every move, but the logical statistics hold it back like iron chains. Yet this time is different. This time I'm not the only one pulling against the chains.

She cares for more than the surface. Even after receiving depth, she wishes to go deeper. This passion is one I retain as well, but the fact that it is being reciprocated is new and intriguing. My heart reaches to others and my intentions are pure, but it is not those she questions, but where they are from. She wants to know the mechanics behind the clock, the artist behind the painting. These are things I find immensely valuable, yet never get the chance to reveal. But here she is, breaking every preconceived notion and painting a new path for how I see the world.

Yet as perfect as she is, the possibilities of a relationship seem to be anything but. Every worldly aspect seems to be telling us no. Every logical requirement seems to be unfulfilled. However, as much as the world is telling us no, it seems as if God is telling us yes. Usually my pursuit of a woman seems to be the opposite, but now that it's right why am I having trouble?

Yes, there are others for both of us. She speaks of another man, an addition to the situation that has been the downfall of many previous endeavors and usually a point of conflict. There are other women wanting to be a part of my life, yet even as I talk to them, it seems as if she is in the back of mind, the one I must pursue. That the woman in front of me is not what I need, but a distraction from the real one I need, her.

I desire the same as her. Someone to hold. Someone to have. Someone to share. Someone to pursue with. And one day someone to love. Do I deserve this? Probably not. Yet God's grace is consistent. Relationships often seem like a house of cards, yet often it is because the base is not secure, it is shaken. Yet the foundation of this new prospect is a foundation that can never be shaken, a foundation in Christ.

The future may seem scary, but we are told to ask for our daily bread. Not our weekly, not our monthly. The house of cards might fall over a week from now or 10 years from now, but we have it today, and it is to be taken in, appreciated, and valued. Tomorrow brings worries of itself. Our only long-term commitment is to Christ, all else falls subject. I don't know if all will go as desired, but I know that God gives and He gives with reason. We may not know what that is, or how to use His gift correctly, but the worst we can do is to ignore the gift all together.

All cards blow over when apart from Christ. Maybe these cards are stronger than our worst fears and are largest worries. Maybe it is not to show the power of our feelings and love, but the power of God's. I don't know what that means for me or her. But I know I'm willing to say yes.

# The Interview
January 30, 2018

"Please State your name and basic information"

"Austin Lanning, 18 years old, born in Waco, Texas."

He presses his hands to the table and peers into my eyes. "I know more than you think I do. I know growing up no one gave a damn about you. I know you're the odd man out in every room. I know the words that stay pierced in your side to this day. I know that everyone thought you were weak, annoying, a stain on this world, a boy that would amount to nothing. Some even thought you were gay. Yet, you knew inside you were none of those things. That everything that anyone ever said about you was false. Yet their accusations drew you to embarrassing situations. I have files here on every drastic attempt to gain acceptance: a song from fifth grade, that afternoon in sixth grade you cried for two hours straight, that time in seventh grade you sat in the bathtub listening to Eminem for four hours contemplating drowning yourself. How about that time in eighth grade you stood on that chair with a noose strung to your ceiling fan staring it in face trying to will yourself to finish it. How about freshman year when you had to learn to walk again and had everything taken away. How about sophomore year when you tried to drive your car into a tree. How about-"

"SHUT UP"

"Oh, you're angry now are you. That's the Austin I know. Let's see that wrath of yours."

I shift back, taking a deep breath. "No, that's not me. That isn't me anymore."

"Why not? Why do you do what you do? Why do you love everyone when still no one gives a damn? Why do you cross oceans for people that don't cross creeks? Why do you stick your neck out for those that try to chop it?"

I shift uncomfortably.

"Ah, you don't know. Why do you pursue music when everyone tears you down? No one supports your music, no one is ever saying: wow Austin is a great musician. Austin has such a beautiful voice. Why do you stay at it?"

I remain in silence.

"You're never the kids' favorites when you save every dime you earn to go see them across the world. You invest tons of time into this acting, yet you can't deny the liberal atmosphere is not your home. Your words that receive praise can't save everyone like you want or at least they couldn't save-"

"STOP"

He laughs. "Oh you want me to stop? That's cute. It's not my fault not even your parents have faith in your endeavors. It's not my fault you have a million people that consider themselves your friends yet haven't been there for you in the slightest. It's not my fault public school has been a hell for you. It's not my fault no teacher appreciates you or understands you. It's not my fault no girl wants you or wants to be with you and if they do you turn them away. It's not my fault you have crazy adventures and ideas that in the end leave you with just yourself. So Austin, you know all this is true, you've felt this, so why? Why keep going?"

"I-I"

He cuts me off. "Just give in. Lighten up. Everyone around you is drinking, smoking, having sex, and living their lives, and guess what? They're not alone. They'll still find success. When will you realize this path your on is meant to fall apart. Just give in. You've done all this to yourself. Just-"

"No."

"What's that?"

"I said no. I don't know why I do what I do, all I know is I'm following Christ. Every single thing you've said is absolutely true. And I know that that's only half of it. Maybe less. And the failures and scars run even further and deeper than that. But I'm a part of something greater than myself. So I have to keep on."

"That's great. Really is. But one day these burdens will become too strong. You can't carry the weight of this world by yourself. And when it crushes you, which it will, I'll be here to laugh and say I told you so. And if this really is your identity, then who are you? Who is Austin Lanning?"

I remain in silence. I don't have an answer.

"ANSWER ME. ANSWER ME YOU NO GOOD, WORTHLESS, FLAWED, MEANINGLESS-"

My fist thrusts forward. My knuckles shatter the glass in front of me. I look up into the broken mirror, the broken reflection of myself. I look down at the blood on my knuckles, and fall to my knees in tears, unable to escape the eternal prosecution within me.

## Stages
February 15, 2018

"I have been here for 4 years now. Not on this island in particular but going from island to island. I think I have been on this one for around 11 months. The one before that... I think I was on it for a year and a half.

On each island I land on, I seem to face a battle of some sort. Sometimes it has been me versus others. Other times it was me versus one individual. And on the occasion, it is me versus myself, in a fight for a sanity and the hope to go on.

Occasionally I will reap a reward from the battles. Everything from food and basic comfort, to entertainment and luxury. And on the very rare occasion, I receive a special gift of love. That one is the best.

I find that sadly I'm not able to enjoy my rewards much anymore. Now that I have become aware of the cycle I am in, I know that soon rewards will leave, I will leave my victory, and I will be issued to a new island with new challenges. It seems so pointless.

I have just come out of a trial and received no reward this time around. I don't know who put me here or is causing this, but I've had enough. I'm exhausted. This is my last letter documenting my time in this. Maybe later someone will see this and save themselves a lot of trouble.

Sincerely,
Austin Lanning."

I close the paper and pin it to the inside of the cave I have been residing in. I walk for a few miles until I come to the edge of the cliff. The highest point on the island. I take a deep breath and begin to walk forward. I look once more at the world around me. My front foot hangs in the air.

"Stop!"

A hand grabs the back of my loose shirt and pulls me back to safety.

I turn to the voice to see a well-built man, taller than I, standing on the grass. His long hair tumbles down His shoulders and His eyes radiate wisdom.

"Who are you?"

He smiles. His teeth glitter in the sunlight. "Why, I'm your Maker." I glare at Him utterly confused. "I mean, someone had to put you here and create all of this."

Anger overwhelms my body. "You!" I sprint at Him. Right as I am about to hit Him, He steps to the side, letting me fly by into the grass.

"What the hell! Why? What? Give me more than that!"

He looks down at me as I pick myself up off the ground.

"I guess it is time you put the pieces together. Everyone starts on an island. Everyone has a starting place."

"Whoa, whoa. These islands weren't my starting place. I used to live somewhere."

"I know. But the moment you agreed to follow Me, is the moment you were placed in this. Getting you here was half of it."

"Okay. But why?"

"Look behind you. Is that not the last island you were at?"

I turn around and out in the distance I see the silhouette of a very familiar land mass. I nod my head.

"You haven't been going randomly from island to island, you've been progressively getting closer."

"Closer... to what?"

"The mainland of course! Where there are no trials or battles. There is no insanity or suffering. It's the final destination!"

"Where's everyone else then?"

"They're here, but I have a unique relationship with all of my children, therefore, they are all on different paths. But as you remember on Island 5 and Island 12 you encountered people that helped you, just as on Island 8 you helped another get through. Many are not here yet though, as they haven't even started. You will encounter people and have many come in and out of your life, but at the end of the day this journey is between Me and you."

"If You're with me, then why am I fighting alone every time? Why am I having battles upon battles? Why am I hurting and wanting to give up?"

He laughs. "My son, look at the battles you've been through. I know you are strong, but do you think you could've won every one of them alone. Let Me tell you something: if you had been fighting alone, you wouldn't have made it past the first hurdle. I have been here all along, ensuring you progress as long as you keep trying. That's the key, you have to maintain hope. Once you lose that, you lose everything.

And as for you wanting to give up, you've got to look at the big picture. Remember Island 6?"

I nod my head, recalling the battle.

He continues, "when you fought that battle, you thought it was the worst thing you had ever done. You wanted any way out you could find. You hated your life and situation and everything around you was crumbling.

Now that you're through it, however, what do you think?"

"It wasn't that bad."

"Exactly. Each difficult challenge you face seems like the world is crashing around because that's all that's around you. If your island falls, you feel that you will too, and it's all over and will never get better. That is until you overcome it, which I already showed that you will, and you look back on the occasion and wonder how you could have been so consumed when there was so much more going on and so much ahead."

I smile at this. I actually feel silly for my previous thoughts.

"And right now you're facing the same thing. This whole island to island process is tiring you. You want out. You're exhausted. But I promise you, that once you get to the mainland, all of this will seem like it was nothing."

"If you don't mind me asking, why must we fight at all?"

"Well if there were no trials or obstacles then what would your faith mean? Just as you must gamble the most money to win the most money, you must gamble your whole life to win more life. To not believe in any of this and to stay where you were, now that would be easy! You'd only believe in what you saw, only do what you felt was right, and not concern yourself with others. And at the end of the day you'd die and experience your turmoil after. But you've chosen something greater than what you see and greater than yourself. You've chosen to give your life and fight any battle for something else. And for that you will be rewarded. I tell you now, these bad times, are the beginning of the best."

"What now then?"
"Enjoy your reward. They may not last forever but they are meant to be enjoyed. There are blessings in this life still."
"But I didn't get a reward this time?"
"You're breathing, are you not? Why, that's the best reward you could be given, all material things are second to that."

He waves as He begins to disappear. A wind blows by, taking Him with it. I walk to the cliff edge once more. I sit down, dangling my feet over the edge. I see the past island in front of me and laugh at the old me that was once there. I had come farther than I thought. Tomorrow might be difficult or it may be a blessing, but either way I am one step closer to the mainland.

# A Life Unwanted
April 14, 2018

I stand before the crowd of people that have become all to familiar to me. These are faces that I have known as long as I can remember. They are faces I share great memories with and have become a part of me. They are faces that have beat me down until I cried. They are faces that have made me question my worth a million times over.

I know what I should do. I need to continue loving. I need to keep following the path. But everything inside me is tearing apart. I become overwhelmed with frustration and pain.

"Every person in this crowd has told me they loved me. They told me they cared. They expect me to do everything in this world for them. Whenever it's advantageous to you, you say you know me, you say I'm a friend. You think it's cool to associate yourself with me. You expect me to bend over backwards for you.

And I have. I've given everything I have to you all. I've cared for each of you more than you know. I've poured out myself for you to walk on and prayed every night that each of you would start making better choices and gain a life of fulfillment. But these words, these words you have told me.."

I begin to cry.

"You guys don't mean any of them. Every night I go home empty. I spend my days pouring into you guys and receive nothing back and I am empty. You guys say you love me, you guys don't give a damn about me! You couldn't care less. Not once have any of you ever told me what I've meant to you. And if you have, you sure as hell didn't mean it. Soon I'll be gone. I'll have left this place. And I won't see a single one of you for the rest of my life because the truth is, none of you are going to make the effort. You expect me to do everything. You expect me to be a safety net when life doesn't turn out just right. You take and take and take and take and then shove me to the ground when you're done.

I spend every day on the outside looking in. Because of you all I often hate who I am. Because of you all I often feel abandoned and neglected. Because of you all I lose the desire to live. The only reason I've lived this far is because I hope the next stage will be better. If it's not then you all can see me at my funeral.

It's amazing I haven't resorted to alcohol or drugs by now. I just desperately cling to God's feet praying He will give me the strength to endure this or God willing, an actual friend. Someone who's word means something.

I'm tired. I'm exhausted. I can't do this anymore. I'm tired of it all. I can't-"

I fall to the ground in tears and exhaustion. I lay there for moments. I gather up the strength to sit up. I look out and the crowd is gone. They had left the minute I began, and one by one disappeared. I fall back down to the ground and resume crying in hopes that the water will take away the pain with it.

# My Prayer Pt.2
April 15, 2018

Dear God,

This is the path I've chosen. I can't be upset at the things that I find on it. You promised me eternal life, eternal love, and eternal fulfillment. But you never said it would be easy.

I have much to learn. I know there are many trials to come. Sadness, on a level I can't even comprehend. There will be frustration that will want to consume me with rage. There will be pain, that I can do nothing with but must lie in. But it's what I signed up for.

All I can ask of You, Lord, is that You get me through the day. I don't justify my anger or frustrations, but I present myself as I am: human and broken. I ask that even when I don't have the strength to put myself back together again that You mend my wounds and support my life in Your hands until I find the will to continue.

Your days hold purpose. The past holds understanding, the present holds opportunity, and the future holds hope. I ask that I don't lose those. I know this won't be the last time I cry out to You in pain. I know this won't be the last time I don't understand. I know this won't be the last time I feel like I'm drowning. But I ask that when I experience it again I have grown. That I have found a little more strength in You. That I have found a little more peace in myself. That I acknowledge the love that never wavered in the first place.

After all, this is the life Your Son, Jesus, lived. He endured more than I ever will. On a daily basis I claim to be a Christian, and to want to be a better one. But if I truly mean that, and I believe I do, it means I am desiring further testing and opposition. I am desiring a life on a narrow path caring for others that will never

understand, a lifestyle no one will fully appreciate or comprehend. But I know it is worth it. You are worth it.

My heart is heavy, but hopeful.
Lord please lift this burden off of me, and let me remember Your
faithfulness.
Lord get me through today. That is my prayer.
No.
Let me rejoice in today. THAT is my prayer.

Your Son,
Austin

# Dear Past Me
May 22, 2018

It's been a journey my friend. I wish you could see where you are now. You're not famous, you're not rich, you're not going D1 in sports. In fact, you've had three knee surgeries, concussions, shoulder injuries, and everything in between since you first wrote yourself. But don't get discouraged. Getting injured was the best thing to ever happen to you as it showed you where to go. It gave you a push you needed.

You're still not in a relationship, but here's the crazy thing: you're okay with it. You've had girls enter and exit your life, but you've learned how to trust God with your life and don't live to find someone. Since then you've become happier and know what you want in a woman.

You're not going to Baylor to become a doctor or a businessman. You're going eleven hours away to Nashville to follow God's call. People laugh at your majors and make fun of your pursuit, but stay confident, I have a feeling it's going to work out just fine.

You've lost people. You're going to hurt like you never have before and the community around you is going to need you. Everything you've done will be used in those moments. You're not going to understand why it all had to happen like it did but nonetheless God will be you're only salvation.

You're going to have friends drop off. People aren't going to understand your pursuit in Christ. They'll get left behind. Don't worry though, they'll figure it out on their own time. Just keep pouring into them no matter how much they reject you. You're pretty good at it actually.

The depression will carry with you. You're going to resort back to old habits. Your heart will hurt. Life is going to get dark. Just remember who you serve and what you're living for and you'll be just fine.

Now that's all negative. Let's get to what's important.

You've found untapped talents. Choir and theatre are going to become a big part of your life. Music will become a passion and acting will become a joy in your life.

God's world is beautiful. You're going to travel to places and do things you've never dreamed. Keep saying yes without hesitation and you'd be surprised the memories you'll make.

Your faith is now number one on the list. It took forever for it to get there, but your faith is growing daily. You just finished pouring into a special group of freshmen for a year, spending four years with a group of guys, leading in the youth, worshipping for children, homeless, and more, and exploring God through K-life and Young Life. If there's anything you need to stick with, it's those communities. They are vital to your growth. You'd be nowhere without them. God is going to change your life. Don't forget to let Him.

Finally, you've become someone you are proud of. I can look back at my years in high school and say that I had no regrets. Let me tell you that's a great feeling. You can look in a mirror now and not become sad or angry. You can walk on a stage and beam with joy at getting the opportunity to share something with someone. You just entered Common Grounds Woodway on the week of your graduation to write this. You're not out with friends. You're not trying to impress people or worrying. You're okay with who you are, passionate about what you're doing, and content with where you're at. It's a beautiful feeling that I don't think you knew you were capable of having. Don't get me wrong there's still a long way to go. Life is just beginning. I'm writing you this to tell you not to give up. Life will continue to be hard and pull you down, that's just the payment of living. But if you keep fighting the good fight and finding the joy in every moment you'll have a much better time. You'll have a more purpose filled time. You'll live a life worth living.

I don't know what the future brings my friend. I really don't. But reflecting on the past years I can bet that if we continue finding new ways to trust God and pursue Him we'll be just fine.

If you do that you'll love others, you'll stay humble, you'll find confidence, you'll worry less, you'll gain respect, you'll live fearlessly, family will become stronger, and everything else will take care of itself.

Don't make the black and white area gray.

Pursue Christ with all that you have.

That's it.

Until we meet again,

You

# FINAL NOTE

I don't think I put everything I wanted to in this book. I don't think that was possible. But, I hope I gave you, as the reader, a seed to grow and find the rest. Although my last journal in the book has ended, as long as I pursue Christ I am sure I will have more to write about. A life lived without others is an empty life and I am grateful to have gotten to share mine with you all. I hope that this book revealed the human condition that we find ourselves suffering from. More than that, I hope that this book revealed that there is hope in that condition; that hope is Christ. Whether it is the fictional life of Eron Basque or the very real life of Austin Lanning, God will prevail in all situations. He has always been faithful and always will be. I pray that you find joy in every moment of this book. In other news, today (June 1st, 2018) is the day I finish writing this chapter of my life. I will send it in to a publisher and hope that it will reach the hearts of those that need it. But, truth be told, if one person can find hope in Christ through this book, it will be success. If you read it and did not, keep searching. I said this was a book about life, not that it covered all of it. Life is more than any arrangement of the 26 letters in our alphabet. Go search for the roots of your pain. Confront the fears you've been running from. Invest yourself in the eternal. There is a breath in your body right now which means God is not yet done with you. There is yet a greater purpose. I wish each of you the best as you find that in your life and pray you will find the hope that has changed my life. May God be with you all.

Till We Meet Again,
-Austin Lanning

Lanning

# ABOUT THE AUTHOR

Austin Lanning is a 19-year-old from Waco, Texas. He currently studies Entertainment Industries and Religious Studies at Belmont University in Nashville, TN. Although this is Austin's first published novel, he is heavily involved in the creative arts. He has two published poems in the National Library of Poetry, several student films, a qualification for Nationals in the International Thespian Society, and soon to be released musical EP.

In addition, his heart is set to serve the world around him and has already participated in many global missions. Thus far he's visited Central and South America, Africa, England, and East Asia. Austin is a Young Life Leader for the Nashville Area. His roots at home run deep in having led children's worship, served in humanity shelters, taught Sunday School, small groups, organized fundraisers, and was runner-up for Rotary Youth Citizen of the Year in 2018.

Austin doesn't know where his life will lead but hopes to use the roses and thorns of his life to further God's Kingdom and to bring hope to all that need it in new and creative ways.

CPSIA information can be obtained
at www.ICGtesting.com
Printed in the USA
LVHW111141280819
629186LV00001BA/53/P